THE LONELY LAKE MONSTER

THE IMAGINARY VETERINARY: BOOK 2

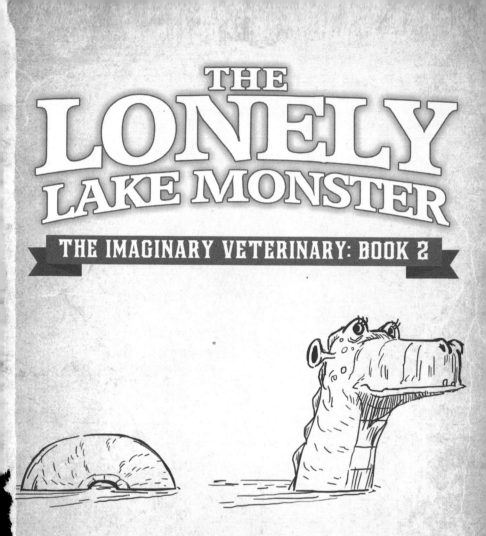

BY SUZANNE SELFORS
ILLUSTRATIONS BY DAN SANTAT

Little, Brown and Company
New York Boston

ALSO BY SUZANNE SELFORS:

The Imaginary Veterinary Series
The Sasquatch Escape
The Lonely Lake Monster

The Smells Like Dog Series
Smells Like Dog
Smells Like Treasure
Smells Like Pirates

To Catch a Mermaid
Fortune's Magic Farm

Text copyright © 2013 by Suzanne Selfors
Illustrations copyright © 2013 by Dan Santat
Text in excerpt from *The Rain Dragon Rescue* copyright © 2013 by Suzanne Selfors
Illustrations in excerpt from *The Rain Dragon Rescue* copyright © 2013 by Dan Santat

Little, Brown and Company

Hachette Book Group
237 Park Avenue, New York, NY 10017
Visit our website at www.lb-kids.com

Little, Brown and Company is a division of Hachette Book Group, Inc.
The Little, Brown name and logo are trademarks of Hachette Book Group, Inc.

The publisher is not responsible for websites (or their content) that are not owned by the publisher.

First Edition: September 2013

Library of Congress Cataloging-in-Publication Data

Selfors, Suzanne.
  The lonely lake monster / by Suzanne Selfors ; illustrations by Dan Santat.—1st ed.
    p. cm.—(The imaginary veterinary ; bk. 2)
  Summary: "Ten-year-olds Pearl and Ben find excitement in the small town of Buttonville as they encounter otherworldly animals, including a lake monster, during their first official day as apprentices to Dr. Woo, a veterinarian for Imaginary Creatures"—Provided by publisher.
  ISBN 978-0-316-22567-0
  [1. Imaginary creatures—Fiction. 2. Veterinarians—Fiction. 3. Apprentices—Fiction.] I. Santat, Dan, ill. II. Title.
  PZ7.S456922Lon 2013
  [Fic]—dc23

2012040967

10 9 8 7 6 5 4 3 2 1

RRD-C

Printed in the United States of America

For lake monsters everywhere

CONTENTS

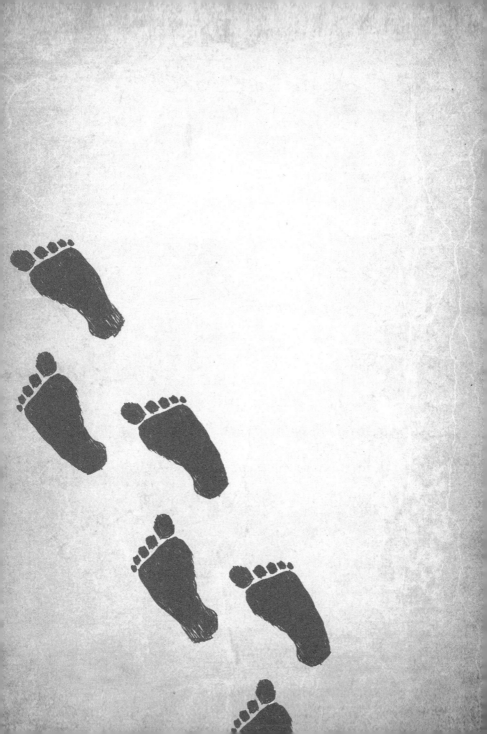

1

Pearl smacked the alarm clock until the loud beeping stopped.

Is it morning already? she thought.

As she rolled over, something crinkled. She rubbed sleep crystals from the corners of her eyes, then rolled the other way. *Crinkle, crinkle.* What was that? Reaching under her pillow, she pulled out a piece of paper.

She still couldn't believe it hadn't been a dream.

What Pearl Petal held in her hand was a certificate of merit in the art of Sasquatch Catching.

That's right. Sasquatch Catching. And it was signed by Dr. Emerald Woo, Veterinarian for Imaginary Creatures.

This was not the usual kind of thing found under a ten-year-old's pillow—like a comic book or a blue jay feather or a secret diary. But last weekend hadn't been a usual kind of weekend. Last weekend, Pearl met an escaped sasquatch. A real, living, breathing, furry, smelly sasquatch. And, being a clever girl, Pearl captured the sasquatch and returned it to Dr. Woo's hospital for Imaginary creatures. That was when she earned the certificate of merit. She'd done such a good job that Dr. Woo had made her an apprentice at the hospital. Today was going to be the first day of the apprenticeship. Maybe Pearl would meet a centaur or a fairy. Perhaps she'd meet a unicorn!

Susan Petal, Pearl's mother, walked into the room, a basket of folded laundry balanced against her hip. "Wake up, sleepyhead."

Pearl quickly tucked the paper under the blanket. As Mrs. Petal opened a dresser drawer, Pearl's

mind raced. Where could she hide her certificate? Beneath the mattress was too obvious. Where, where, where?

"What time are you supposed to be at Dr. Woo's?"

"Eight o'clock," Pearl said. She'd set the alarm for 7 AM to be certain she'd have plenty of time to get ready. She didn't want to be late for her first day.

"Are you sure you want to do this?" Mrs. Petal dropped three pairs of rolled socks into the top drawer. "Your father and I still expect you to get your chores done."

Pearl stiffened. "Yes, I'm sure. I'm totally sure. I really, really, *really* want to be an apprentice." She blew a lock of blond hair from her face.

"I don't understand why you're so excited about working at a *worm* hospital," Mrs. Petal said with a shake of her head.

Because it's not really a worm hospital, Pearl thought. But she couldn't say that. The sign on the hospital's gate read DR. WOO'S WORM HOSPITAL, but that was a big fat lie. No one was supposed to know that Dr. Woo worked with Imaginary creatures. Pearl had found out only because of the sasquatch incident, and afterward, she'd signed a contract of secrecy.

"Worms are cool," Pearl said.

"Cool?" Mrs. Petal opened another drawer and looked tenderly at her daughter. "Well, I guess working in a worm hospital is something to do. I know you get bored in the store all day. Your father thinks this apprenticeship might keep you out of trouble." Her gaze darted to the newspaper article that was framed and mounted on Pearl's wall. FIRE DEPARTMENT RESCUES GIRL STUCK IN TREE—AGAIN!

Pearl frowned. She didn't get into trouble on purpose, and she certainly didn't keep a troublemaking list. But Buttonville was a very boring town. Many of the shops had closed down, along with the bowling alley and the toy store. Most of the young families had moved away. There was almost nothing to do, so Pearl had to be clever. It wasn't her fault that other people didn't like some of her clever ideas.

"I was trying to get a woodpecker's nest," she reminded her mother. "I didn't need the fire department. I know how to climb out of a tree."

WARNING

"Well, it's too bad Dr. Woo runs a worm hospital and not a bird hospital. You could show the doctor your lovely nest collection." Mrs. Petal tucked T-shirts into the drawer, then closed it. "Don't forget to eat your breakfast before you leave." Laundry basket in hand, she left the bedroom.

As her mother's footsteps faded, Pearl threw her blanket aside and scrambled out of bed. Her corner shelf was cluttered with old board games. She opened the lid to a game called Pot O'Gold. The golden pot was filled with plastic playing pieces—leprechauns, gold coins, and rainbows. What a perfect hiding place. No one in her family had played

Pot O'Gold in years. She stuck the certificate of merit into the golden pot and set the lid back on top. Then she ran to the bathroom.

Five minutes to shower, five minutes to dress, five minutes to eat breakfast. That would leave plenty of time to walk to Dr. Woo's. Soon she'd begin her apprenticeship. Her scalp tingled with excitement.

What wondrous creature would she meet today?

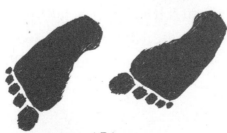

2

LEMON FACE

Pearl had no idea what an apprentice should wear, so she selected her usual clothes—a pair of shiny basketball shorts that hung below her knees, a plain cotton T-shirt, and a pair of sneakers. The shorts were navy, the shirt was white, and the sneakers had once been white but, after five months of wear, were now the color of mud and starting to fall apart. She pulled her long blond hair into a ponytail because she liked the way it felt when it swayed back and forth. Besides, if her hair was hanging in her face, she might miss seeing something at Dr. Woo's. And that would be a shame.

Her breakfast plate sat on the table. The scrambled eggs, toast, and ham were still warm. Using all three ingredients, Pearl created a breakfast sandwich, something she liked to do whenever possible. Eating a sandwich for lunch was normal, but Pearl enjoyed them for breakfast and dinner, too. Spaghetti sandwiches were delicious and much easier to eat than trying to spin the long noodles onto a fork. Meatballs made great sandwiches, as did tuna noodle casserole, scalloped potatoes, and her all-time favorite, french fries and ketchup.

As she chewed, her parents' muffled voices drifted up the stairs. The Petals lived above the Dollar Store, which they owned and operated. It was one of the few shops still open in the little town of Buttonville. In the old days, most everyone in Buttonville had worked at the button factory, creating handmade buttons that were sold all over the world. But no one worked there anymore. Cheap, plastic buttons had become more popular than the exotic kind once produced at the Buttonville factory—buttons made

from materials like cedar, porcelain, and oyster shell. For the last five years, the factory had been vacant. The lawn had grown into a weed-infested field, the windows had darkened with dirt, and the concrete walls had become drizzled in pigeon droppings.

But Dr. Woo had recently taken over the old building. She lived there now, along with creatures Pearl used to think could be found only in storybooks— not at the edge of her hometown!

She finished the breakfast sandwich, drank a glass of milk, then hurried downstairs to the Dollar Store.

Pearl's parents were busy unpacking boxes that had recently been delivered. They both wore green aprons embroidered with the slogan **YOU GET MORE AT THE DOLLAR STORE**. Pearl's apron hung on a hook near the cash register. She wouldn't need it today.

Pearl's father, Peter Petal, pulled a pair of yellow flip-flops from a box. "Look. Just in time for the nice weather." Then he held up a blue pair. "These are your size."

"Great," Pearl said. She kicked off her sneakers and slid her feet into the rubber shoes. They fit perfectly. And they matched her blue shorts.

"The mirrors came in," Mrs. Petal said as she peeled open a different box. Inside lay dozens of plastic mirrors, some big enough to hang on a wall, some small enough to tuck into a purse. This was the best part of owning the Dollar Store. Boxes arrived a few times a week, filled with all sorts of things—tubes of toothpaste, striped socks, glitter pens, sometimes even chocolate. Pearl could keep whatever she wanted. "Why don't you give this one to Lemon Face," Mrs. Petal said as she held out a tiny pink mirror.

In her rush to get to Dr. Woo's, Pearl had almost forgotten to feed the bird. She grabbed the pink mirror and opened the cage. "Hi, Lemon Face." The yellow parakeet was busy looking into a silver mirror that Pearl had given him a few months ago. She clipped the pink mirror to the cage, then filled the seed and water trays. Lemon Face scuttled to the end of his perch and began to twitter at his reflection in the new mirror. "He seems happy," Pearl said as the parakeet bobbed his head and sang a little song.

"He thinks he's made a new friend." Mr. Petal opened another box, this one filled with greeting cards. "That's why he stands there all day and talks to his reflection."

Pearl shrugged. It made sense, especially since Lemon Face's brain was about the size of half a chickpea. "I'm glad you like your new friend," she told him. Then she closed the cage and glanced up at the clock. 7:30. "Oh, I gotta go. See ya."

"Hold on, young lady." Mrs. Petal removed her Dollar Store apron and grabbed her purse. "I'm going with you."

"Huh?" Pearl whipped around. "Why?"

"I need to meet Dr. Woo before I give permission for you to work as her apprentice."

Pearl nervously tapped her toes against the flip-flops. "You don't need to meet her. She's real nice. I promise."

"Your mother needs to meet her," Mr. Petal said as he began to set the greeting cards into a rack. "We can't let you spend the day with someone we haven't met."

Pearl frowned. "But..." The hospital was a secret. Parents weren't allowed inside. No one was allowed inside. Dr. Woo wouldn't like this. "But..."

★13★

"What are you waiting for?" Mrs. Petal asked as she held open the Dollar Store's front door. She smiled her gap-toothed smile, which perfectly matched Pearl's gap-toothed smile. "You don't want to be late on your first day, do you?"

Pearl shook her head. How would she explain this to Dr. Woo? How would she keep her mother from trying to get inside the hospital?

Was her apprenticeship over before it had even begun?

3

BAD BERRIES

As Pearl and her mother walked down Main Street, Pearl's flip-flops smacked against the sidewalk, the rhythm echoing off the brick buildings. Sunshine sparkled in the morning sky. A gray squirrel scrambled up a lamppost. A pair of pigeons flew out of the way. "Pearl, slow down," her mother called after her.

"I don't want to be late," she answered, her ponytail swinging with each eager step.

"And I don't want to twist my ankle." Mrs. Petal waved at Mr. Bundle, an old man who was sitting on a bench outside the Buttonville Barbershop. He scowled and didn't wave back, most likely because he hadn't forgiven Pearl for riding her bike over his foot earlier that year. She'd been trying to follow a butterfly and hadn't noticed the outstretched limb. He'd limped for two whole months.

Pearl passed right by Ms. Nod, who was unlocking the door to the Buttonville Bookstore. "Hello," Mrs. Petal greeted as she approached.

Ms. Nod peered over the rims of her red glasses. "I have not changed my mind," she said, blocking the doorway with her outstretched arms. "Pearl is still banned."

Pearl hadn't meant to get banned from the bookstore. But there was no sign in the store that read DON'T CLIMB THE BOOKSHELVES. How was she supposed to know that if one bookshelf tipped, the rest would fall like dominos?

"Well, I hope you'll change your mind," Mrs. Petal told Ms. Nod. "Pearl certainly loves your bookstore."

As she continued down the street, Mrs. Petal greeted everyone she passed. But Pearl didn't bother to say hello to anyone. She was in a hurry. And besides, some days it felt as if the entire town was mad at her for something or other. "She's a troublemaker," people would whisper behind her back. Pearl thought it wasn't fair to call someone a troublemaker when that someone didn't get into trouble on purpose.

But Dr. Woo wasn't mad at Pearl and didn't think Pearl was a troublemaker. And that was all the more reason why Pearl wanted to arrive on time.

With her mother close behind, Pearl charged around the corner and headed up Fir Street. A car driving toward them suddenly turned into a parking spot, its tires screeching. The driver's window opened, and a woman stuck out her head. "Yoo-hoo! Yoo-hoo!"

Pearl knew that voice. The sound was worse than fingernails on a chalkboard, worse than a cat

upchucking a hair ball, worse than a dentist's drill. It was a voice that left scratch marks in the air.

It belonged to Mrs. Martha Mulberry, Buttonville's busiest busybody. She squeezed through the car window until she was half hanging out, her red hair dangling in long, frizzy ropes. "Where are you two going this morning?"

"Nowhere," Pearl said, not slowing down. It was best not to talk to Mrs. Mulberry. That woman could smell a secret ten miles away. And once she uncovered a secret, she never kept it. In fact, Mrs. Mulberry gave secrets away as if they were pieces of candy on Halloween.

"Nowhere?" Mrs. Mulberry narrowed her eyes. "Clearly you are going *somewhere*."

"We're going to meet Dr. Woo," Mrs. Petal said.

Pearl skidded to a stop. *Drat!* Her mother had spilled the beans.

"Dr. Woo?" Mrs. Mulberry squeezed back into the car, threw open the door, then scrambled out. Dressed in red overalls, she looked like a huge radish. She hurried up to Mrs. Petal and stood facing

her, hands perched on hips. "Why are you going to meet Dr. Woo?"

Before Mrs. Petal could answer, Pearl pushed between the two women. "No reason," she said. "Just a friendly visit." She grabbed her mother's arm and tried to pull her down the sidewalk. But Mrs. Mulberry stood in the way.

"If you are going to meet Dr. Woo, then I must go with you," Mrs. Mulberry said.

"No way," Pearl blurted. "You can't go with us."

"Don't be rude," Mrs. Petal whispered to her daughter.

"Can't go with you? That's absurd," Mrs. Mulberry said. "I've been trying to meet Dr. Woo ever since I learned that she'd moved into the old button factory. As president of the Welcome Wagon, it is my job to welcome her to town." She pointed to the words WELCOME WAGON, which were embroidered on the front of her red baseball cap. "I tried to get in on Saturday, and then again on Sunday, but the gate was locked. I yelled her name, but no one answered. Then I heard a strange noise coming from the old factory. It sounded like a growl."

It probably was a growl, Pearl thought. *A sasquatch growl.* But how could she keep Mrs. Mulberry from suspecting such a thing?

"Dogs growl," Pearl pointed out. "Maybe someone's dog was on the loose. Or maybe it wasn't a growl after all. Maybe it was a branch swaying in the wind."

"Growl or no growl, I'm going with you," Mrs. Mulberry insisted.

Mrs. Mulberry would ruin everything. Dr. Woo was trying to keep her hospital for Imaginary creatures a secret. What if Mrs. Mulberry pushed her way in? She was a very pushy person. And what if she caught a glimpse of an Imaginary creature? "You can't go with us, because we have an appointment and you don't," Pearl said, jutting out her chin.

"An appointment?" Mrs. Mulberry leaned close to Pearl. Her breath smelled like coffee. "Why do *you* have an appointment with Dr. Woo?"

Before Pearl could come up with a fake reason,

Mrs. Petal smiled proudly and said, "Dr. Woo has asked Pearl to be her apprentice."

Mrs. Mulberry snorted. "Why would Dr. Woo want Pearl to be her apprentice? Doesn't she know that Pearl is a...*difficult* child?"

Mrs. Petal's smile faded. She wrapped her arm around her daughter's shoulders and glared at Mrs. Mulberry. "She's not a difficult child. She's a wonderful child."

"Wonderful?" Mrs. Mulberry snorted again. "*Wonderful* children do not ring the Town Hall bell at the crack of dawn."

"I wanted to see if the dogs would start howling," Pearl explained.

"*Wonderful* children do not leave puddles of ice cream on the sidewalk," Mrs. Mulberry said.

"I was trying to see which flavor melted fastest," Pearl pointed out.

"*Wonderful* children do not cut the roses off other people's rosebushes."

"I said I was sorry," Pearl told her, having no

exceptional explanation for that particular behavior. She'd simply wanted some flowers for her mother. "We gave you a new rosebush."

"A Dollar Store rosebush can never replace a rosebush from a gardening catalog," Mrs. Mulberry said with a roll of her eyes.

Mrs. Petal's cheeks turned red. "You have a right to your opinion, Martha, but your opinion is wrong. Dr. Woo thinks Pearl is wonderful, and so do I. Now, please move out of the way. We do not want to be late."

But Mrs. Mulberry didn't budge. And when Mrs. Petal tried to step around her, she blocked the way again. "If Pearl gets to be an apprentice, then my daughter should get to be an apprentice, too. *Victoria!*"

The backseat window of Mrs. Mulberry's car rolled down, and Victoria Mulberry peered out. "What?" she asked, pushing her thick glasses up her nose.

Pearl groaned. Victoria Mulberry was her least favorite person in the world. She'd spent most of her life tattling on Pearl. And she'd never invited Pearl to one of her birthday parties.

"Victoria, sweetie?" Mrs. Mulberry called. "Would you like to be an apprentice for Dr. Woo?"

"No."

"But Pearl is going to be an apprentice for Dr. Woo."

"I don't care." Sunlight glinted off Victoria's blue braces.

Mrs. Mulberry stomped over to the car. "Listen to me, Victoria Bernice Mulberry. I want to know why Dr. Woo keeps that gate locked and why no one has seen her. And I want to know what really made that growling sound. I think she's hiding something, and I don't like it when people try to hide things from me. If you work as her apprentice, then you can help me find out what's going on."

"I don't want to."

"Well, I am your mother and I want you to." Mrs. Mulberry scrambled back into the driver's seat. "We'll go home, and you can change into that pretty pink dress, the one you wore when you accepted

the Buttonville Welcome Wagon student-of-the-year award. And then we will demand that Dr. Woo meet you and give you an apprenticeship."

Welcome Wagon student of the year? Pearl snorted. *More like Welcome Wagon pest of the year.*

As the car drove away, Victoria glared at Pearl as if the whole thing was Pearl's fault.

"That is a horrid woman," Mrs. Petal said. "But you are a wonderful girl." And she kissed Pearl's cheek.

"Come on," Pearl urged as she pointed at her plastic Dollar Store watch. "It's almost eight o'clock."

4

A BOY
NAMED BEN

The old button factory stood at the edge of town. The ten-story, concrete building loomed behind a wrought-iron fence. Last week, Pearl had watched a giant bird fly toward the factory—a bird that bore an amazing resemblance to a dragon. But at that moment, the only thing flying overhead was a lone pigeon.

A long gravel driveway led from the entry gate to the factory's front door. The gate was secured with a chain and padlock. It had been that way ever since the factory closed down.

Pearl, in her constant search for something to do, had climbed over the fence many times. She'd searched the overgrown grass for stray buttons. Buttons could be found all over Buttonville, thanks to the birds that had snatched them from the factory, year after year, to decorate their nests. The prettiest one Pearl had discovered was shaped like a heart and made from mother-of-pearl. The strangest one looked like a glass eyeball. But Pearl's trespassing had been outdoors only. Even though there were plenty of broken windows to crawl through, she'd never gone inside the vacant building. It was dark in there, and the wind made an eerie sound as it snaked between cracks in the glass. After a while, she'd lost interest in the old factory. But then she'd met a boy named Ben. And that was when everything changed.

Ben Silverstein, age ten, had arrived in Buttonville just four days ago. He'd come all the way from Los Angeles, California, to stay with his grandfather, Abe Silverstein. The reason Pearl and Ben had first visited Dr. Woo's hospital was because

Ben had found a dragon hatchling on his bed. His grandfather's black cat, Barnaby, had captured the little creature. The hatchling's wing was torn, and green blood oozed from its cat-bite wound. Pearl and Ben had taken it to the hospital for care, and that was when the whole sasquatch adventure began. Ben had earned a Sasquatch Catching certificate and was going to be an apprentice, too. He seemed nice enough, but other kids had seemed nice and then turned out to be mean. Pearl needed more time before she truly knew if Ben was her friend.

Pearl and her mother crossed the street and headed for the factory's gate. Ben and his grandfather were already there.

"Hi, Pearl," Ben said. He stuck his hands into his pants pockets. They were the kind of jeans that came with a fancy label. And his sneakers were brand-new, without a smudge or a stain. A famous basketball player's name was stamped on the backs. Shoes like that didn't come from the Dollar Store.

"My mom wants to meet Dr. Woo," Pearl whispered to Ben.

"My grandfather wants to meet her, too," Ben whispered back.

Grandpa Abe leaned on his wooden cane, the summer sun reflecting off his bald head. "So, what do you think about this?" He pointed to the sign that hung from the gate.

WELCOME TO DR. WOO'S WORM HOSPITAL.

DR. WOO DOES NOT TREAT CATS, DOGS, PIGS, RATS, SNAKES, TURTLES, FISH, FROGS, OR ANY OTHER CREATURE THAT IS NOT A WORM. DR. WOO SEES WORMS BY APPOINTMENT ONLY. IF YOU DON'T HAVE AN APPOINTMENT,

KEEP OUT!

"I think it's very odd," Mrs. Petal said after reading the sign. "I don't know anyone who has a pet worm. Why would Buttonville need a worm hospital?"

"Buttonville needs a worm hospital as much as I need a hole in my head," Grandpa Abe said with a chuckle. "But Ben is very excited. Who knew? My grandson, the worm apprentice."

"I could barely sleep," Pearl told Ben. "What do you think we'll do on our first day?"

"I don't know, but I brought some bandages, just in case." He patted his back pocket. Then he held out his shiny wristwatch. "It's almost time. Only one more minute."

They wrapped their fingers around the bars and stared through the gate. Even though they were the same age, Pearl stood a head taller than Ben. And while her long hair was the color of wheat, Ben's was dark and cropped super short. "My heart is bouncing around like a Mexican jumping bean," she said.

"Mine, too." He gripped the bars tighter. "I keep thinking about that form we signed. The one that said we could get stomped or crushed."

"Shhh," Pearl warned. "If my mom hears about

that form, I'll never get to be an apprentice."

During Ben's and Pearl's first visit to the hospital, they'd each signed a form agreeing that they wouldn't blame Dr. Woo if they got hurt. There'd been a long list of ways this could happen—biting, stomping, crushing, and shredding, to name a few. But Pearl wasn't worried. She knew how to take care of herself. Ben, however, didn't look so confident. His forehead glistened with sweat, and he chewed on his lower lip. He looked like he might turn and run.

"Don't be scared," she told him. She pulled two pieces of gum from her pocket, shoved one in her mouth, and offered the other to Ben. He popped it into his mouth. "We'll be okay."

"I'm not scared," he said, standing as tall as he could. "I just think we should be careful." He checked his watch again. "It's eight o'clock."

Pearl looked over her shoulder. Mrs. Mulberry's car was nowhere to be seen. Hopefully, it would take Victoria a very long time to change into her pink dress—long enough for Pearl and Ben to get safely inside the hospital without Mrs. Mulberry bothering Dr. Woo.

"Look." Ben nudged Pearl with his elbow. Her gaze rolled down the long driveway and rested on the front door, which was slowly opening.

A woman stepped out.

"Dr. Woo," Pearl whispered.

5

WORM DOCTOR

There she stood in her white lab coat, her long black hair cascading over her shoulders like a river of ink. She looked down the driveway and waved. Pearl bounced on her flip-flops and waved back. This was it. Her mother would meet Dr. Woo and Ben's grandfather would meet Dr. Woo and they'd see what a nice person she was. Then Pearl and Ben would go inside and begin their apprenticeships. And it would be the best summer ever.

Dr. Woo walked with small, graceful steps. A

stethoscope hung from her neck, its silver bell sparkling in the sun. No one said a word. The only sound was a quiet *crunch, crunch* as the soles of the doctor's shoes pressed into the gravel. When she reached the gate, she pulled a ring of keys from her coat pocket and unlocked the padlock. After the gate swung open, she stepped out.

"Hello," she said, her voice calm and soft. "I am Dr. Emerald Woo." She held out her hand to Mrs. Petal. Her right index finger was missing.

"Hello. I'm Susan Petal, Pearl's mother."

"And I'm Abe Silverstein, Ben's grandfather." Grandpa Abe also shook the doctor's hand. "Welcome to Buttonville."

"Thank you." A few specks of yellow glitter dotted the doctor's cheekbones. Pearl remembered the glitter that had fallen from Dr. Woo's hair during their first visit to her office. She'd told them it was fairy dust.

"Ben? Pearl? Are you ready to begin?"

"Yes!" they both said as they hurried through the gateway. But Dr. Woo held up a hand when Grandpa

Abe and Mrs. Petal each took a step forward. "I'm sorry, but only employees are allowed on the grounds. Worms are very delicate creatures. They require peace and quiet."

"Really?" Mrs. Petal said. "I never knew that."

Dr. Woo grabbed the gate. "Good day," she said.

"But I thought..." Mrs. Petal frowned. "I mean, I'd like to ask you a few questions."

"So would I," said Grandpa Abe.

Pearl's shoulders slumped. What if Dr. Woo gave an answer they didn't like? Or what if Ben got permission to go inside but Pearl didn't? She chewed her gum doubly fast.

"Questions?" Dr. Woo folded her arms. "Very well."

"Where are you from?" Mrs. Petal asked.

"Iceland."

Pearl wondered if Dr. Woo was telling the truth about Iceland. After all, she'd lied about the hospital being a place for worms. Maybe she was also lying about where she came from.

"I've never heard of a worm hospital," Grandpa Abe said. "What will Ben and Pearl be doing?"

"Cleaning the worm cages, feeding the worms— all things worm-related. Worms are creatures deserving of care just like any other creature." Dr. Woo raised her eyebrows, as if daring them to question her further. "There are thousands of worms living in the dirt, right here on the hospital grounds. And there are hundreds of thousands more, maybe millions, in Buttonville."

"Oh, my, that's a lot of worms," Mrs. Petal said.

"Did you know that there are almost three thousand kinds of worms, and the largest one can grow up to twenty-two feet long?"

"Twenty-two feet long?" Grandpa Abe chuckled. "*Oy gevalt!* Who needs a worm that long?"

Pearl wondered if the twenty-two-foot-long worm was another lie. Or maybe it was one of the Imaginary creatures that Dr. Woo kept in her hospital. *Yuck*, she thought.

"We need both big and small worms," Dr. Woo

told Ben's grandfather with a smile. "Without them, the Known World wouldn't have such lovely dirt."

"Known world?" Grandpa Abe leaned on his cane. "Did you say *known* world?"

Dr. Woo stopped smiling. Her expression turned serious. "I didn't say any such thing. Why would I say *known* world? That would be a strange thing to say."

"I'm pretty sure that's what you said," Mrs. Petal confirmed.

Pearl and Ben shared a look of understanding. They'd heard this term before. While visiting Dr. Woo's hospital a few days ago, they'd been told that there was a Known World and an Imaginary World. Buttonville and Los Angeles were located in the Known World. How, exactly, you got to the Imaginary World was still a mystery—one that Pearl was determined to solve.

A white van drove up and parked, and a young man jumped out. "Delivery for Dr. Woo," he announced, dropping two large boxes on the sidewalk. Then he climbed back into the van and drove off.

"'Kiwi-flavored jelly beans,'" Ben read as he examined the labels.

"Would you be so kind as to collect those?" Dr. Woo asked, motioning to Ben and Pearl. They each picked up a box.

Then Dr. Woo shook the ring of keys. "Well, it's time to begin. The apprentices will be escorted back through the gate at precisely three o'clock." Dr. Woo closed the gate and snapped the padlock into place.

"Why do you keep the gate locked?" Grandpa Abe wondered from the other side of the bars.

"There are only two reasons to lock a gate," Dr. Woo said, lowering her voice as if she was about to tell a secret. Everyone, even Pearl and Ben, leaned as close as possible to hear. "Reason number one— to keep things in."

"What sorts of things?" Grandpa Abe asked.

Dr. Woo hesitated. "Well...the worms, of course. We don't want sick worms leaving the hospital before they are cured. Worms are masters of escape."

Grandpa Abe's mouth fell open. Pearl could guess what he was thinking. *How can a locked gate stop a worm?*

"That makes total sense," Pearl said, trying to be helpful to Dr. Woo.

"It makes no sense," Ben whispered.

"Of course it makes no sense," Pearl whispered back. "But she can't tell your grandfather about not wanting the sasquatch to escape."

"And reason number two?" Mrs. Petal asked the doctor.

"Reason number two—to keep things out. Things like fishermen and birds. They are the enemies of worms."

"Now that makes sense," Mrs. Petal said with a nod.

Dr. Woo tucked the key ring into her coat pocket. "Time is of the essence. If the questions are concluded, I would like to get back to the hospital."

"Okay by me," Grandpa Abe said. "See ya later, Ben."

Mrs. Petal smiled through the bars at Pearl. "Have a nice time. And be sure to call me if you need anything."

Mrs. Petal accepted an offer from Grandpa Abe for a ride back to the Dollar Store. As Pearl and Ben watched the car drive away, they sighed with relief.

"That was close," Pearl said as she and Ben hurried to catch up with Dr. Woo, who was already halfway up the drive. The package Pearl carried wasn't very heavy, even though the label said it contained a thousand fun-sized boxes of jelly beans. "Are you having a party or something?"

"The jelly beans are for the fairies," Dr. Woo replied. "They prefer tropical flavors, such as coconut, pineapple, and mango. But kiwi is their favorite."

Pearl couldn't believe it. "Fairies eat candy?"

"Fairies eat sugar in all its forms. It is their primary source of nourishment." Yellow glitter drifted from the doctor's hair. A few flecks landed on Pearl's box.

"Can I meet a fairy?" she asked.

Dr. Woo didn't respond. She quickened her pace.

"What are we going to do?" Ben asked as they headed up the hospital's front steps. "We're not really going to work with worms, are we?"

"Of course we're not going to work with worms," Pearl said. Then she frowned. "We're not, right?"

Still, Dr. Woo said nothing. Was she always this mysterious?

As they followed the doctor inside, the sound of an engine roared in the distance. Pearl whipped around. Mrs. Mulberry's car screeched to a stop outside the gate.

"Yoo-hoo, Dr. Woo!" Mrs. Mulberry called, scrambling from the car. "I've brought my daughter to meet you. Yoo—"

Pearl didn't waste a second. She dropped the jelly bean box, pushed Ben out of the way, and flung herself at the hospital's front door. Ben lost his balance and fell as Pearl slammed the door shut. *Good riddance, Victoria!* Then she slid the dead bolt into place.

"What did you do that for?" Ben complained as he struggled to his feet.

"I didn't mean to push you over. But Victoria Mulberry is trying to steal my apprentice job."

"I think I broke my tailbone." He rubbed his backside. "We haven't even started and I'm hurt already."

"Sorry," Pearl said. Then she looked around and gasped.

Dr. Woo had disappeared.

6

The hospital lobby was big and empty. Cobwebs crisscrossed the high ceiling. A door marked EMPLOYEES ONLY stood on one side. A door marked IDENTIFICATION ROOM stood on the other side. Both were closed. An elevator waited.

"Where'd Dr. Woo go?" Pearl asked, stepping over her box of jelly beans.

"I don't know," Ben said. He picked up the other box, which had tumbled from his hands when he fell, and set it on top of Pearl's.

"Well, what do we do now?" She didn't want to do

the wrong thing and get into trouble on her first day.

"Maybe we should wait," Ben said with a shrug.

Pearl tapped her feet and popped some bubbles with her gum. Where had the doctor gone? This wasn't fun. The first day of their apprenticeships was supposed to be fun! "I hate waiting," she grumbled. "It feels like forever."

"It's only been a minute," Ben informed her.

"A minute can be a very, very long time." Pearl charged over to the Identification Room door and tried to push it open. "Locked," she reported. Then she checked the Employees Only door. "This one's locked, too." She rapped her knuckles on the door. "Hello? Did you forget about us? Hello?"

Ben pressed his ear to the Employees Only door. "I don't hear anything."

Pearl knocked louder. *"Hello?"*

"Why are you two making such a racket?"

Both Pearl and Ben gasped, surprised by the voice that came from the other side of the lobby. They whipped around. The Identification Room door had opened and an odd-looking man stood in the doorway.

A big grin spread across Pearl's face. "Hi, Mr. Tabby." Both she and Ben knew him. He'd examined the dragon hatchling when they'd brought it to the hospital. He'd told them it was called a wyvern, a special two-legged dragon that grew a barbed tail. He'd also given them a Sasquatch Catching Kit so they could bring the big hairy beast back to the hospital.

Pearl thought Mr. Tabby looked like a butler in his perfectly creased black pants, white shirt, plaid vest, and shiny black shoes. Long red hair was pulled into a ponytail, and a red mustache perched beneath his nose—but it was no ordinary mustache. It was waxed into sections and reminded Pearl of a cat's whiskers. *How much time does it take each morning to do that?* she wondered.

"Do those boxes contain kiwi-flavored jelly beans?" he asked. Pearl and Ben nodded. "I'd find it most helpful if you'd set them in the elevator." Once they'd done this, the doors closed, carrying the boxes upward. The panel above the elevator lit up—floor one, two, three—and stopped on four.

"What's on the fourth floor?" Pearl asked. "Is that where the fairies are?"

Acting as if he hadn't heard the question, Mr. Tabby sniffed the air. "Do I detect an odor of parakeet?" He sniffed Pearl's head. "Yes, indeed I do. Known World variety. Male." His half-moon irises expanded. "Do you own such a creature?"

"Yes," Pearl said. "His name is Lemon Face."

"Parakeets are delicious with mustard." Mr. Tabby said this as if it were normal to eat parakeets with mustard. Pearl frowned and made a mental note to

never, ever let Mr. Tabby near Lemon Face.

"I also detect the odor of fruit-flavored chewing gum. Gum is not allowed on hospital grounds. Please deposit it into the receptacle." He pointed to a small trash can. Both Pearl and Ben spat out their gum.

Then Ben shuffled in place. "Where's Dr. Woo?" he asked.

"Dr. Woo has been called away on an emergency, and therefore, your first day of apprentice training will fall on my shoulders." He stroked a section of his mustache. "It is unfortunate timing, but we must make the best of it."

Pearl didn't know Mr. Tabby very well, but from the short time she'd spent with him, she'd come to the conclusion that he was rather grumpy. What kind of teacher would he make? She opened her mouth to speak, and as she did, a low growl sounded in Mr. Tabby's throat.

"Will your question be of the bothersome variety?" he asked, folding his arms.

"Um..." Pearl screwed up her face. She didn't have one question—she had many. And they weren't

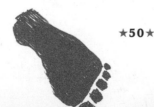

bothersome—they were important. So despite Mr. Tabby's stern look, she went for it. "What kind of emergency did Dr. Woo go on? Did she go to the Imaginary World? Can we go with her? What kind of creature is sick? Can we meet it? Is it going to die? If we are her apprentices, then shouldn't we be with her? Isn't that our job? And—"

"Perhaps you do not know the definition of *bothersome*." Mr. Tabby narrowed his eyes. "Please choose *one* question."

Ben stepped forward. "What are we going to do today?"

"Now that is a question I can answer. Follow me." He strode to the Employees Only door. The last time Pearl and Ben saw Mr. Tabby, a tail had slid out the bottom of his vest. Pearl watched carefully, looking for a hint of the furry appendage, but nothing appeared. She thought about asking him if he had a tail but changed her mind. That was probably *bothersome.*

Mr. Tabby placed his hand on the door, his long fingers spread wide. The door hummed and clicked open.

"It must have read his fingerprints," Ben whispered to Pearl as they followed Mr. Tabby through the doorway. "My dad has a security system at his office that reads fingerprints."

"Cool."

The door closed behind them.

They stood in a hallway. It looked like a regular, boring hallway that could have been in a regular, boring building. But this was a hospital for Imaginary creatures. This hallway should be different. Disappointment settled over Pearl like a wet blanket. Where was the magic? The wonder? Where were the fairies and their dust?

"Pay close attention," Mr. Tabby said. He stood in front of a bulletin board. One side of the board was labeled OFF DUTY, and the other side was labeled ON DUTY. Mr. Tabby removed two cards from the OFF DUTY side. One card had Pearl's name written on it, the other, Ben's name. The remaining card belonged to someone named Vinny.

"These are your time cards," Mr. Tabby explained. "You will clock in when you arrive and clock out when you leave." He took Pearl's card and slid it into a clock that hung next to the bulletin board. A *click* sounded. The day's date and time were now printed at the top of the card. He slid Ben's into the slot, and the same thing happened. Then he pinned each card to the ON DUTY side of the board, next to one labeled MR. TABBY and another labeled VIOLET.

"Who are Violet and Vinny?" Pearl asked.

"Violet and Vinny work for Dr. Woo, and that is all you need to know." Mr. Tabby straightened the time cards so they were perfectly parallel. "It is extremely important that you clock in and out. That is the best way for us to keep track of you. The previous apprentice always forgot to use the time clock and..." He paused. "We lost her."

"What do you mean, you *lost* her?" Ben asked.

Mr. Tabby's upper lip rose in a slight sneer. "Because she neglected to clock in and clock out, we do not know if she disappeared in the Known World or in the Imaginary World."

"Disappeared?" A shiver ran down Pearl's spine. "Are you telling us that she's...missing?"

WARNING

7

SNACKS FOR HUMANS

Mr. Tabby smoothed the front of his plaid vest. "The previous apprentice was here one day, and the next day she wasn't here. And she hasn't been here since." He picked a stray red hair off his sleeve. Ben and Pearl watched it make its slow journey to the floor. "So, yes, she is missing."

"When did this happen?" Pearl asked.

"Some time ago, at our previous hospital location." Mr. Tabby opened a closet door and took out two white lab coats. Then he changed the subject. "Your uniforms."

"Cool." Ben grabbed one and put it on. "This is like the mad-scientist costume I wore for Halloween."

Pearl wanted to ask more questions about the mysterious girl who'd once worked for Dr. Woo, but she couldn't take her eyes off the lab coat. It was so much better than the green apron she wore at the Dollar Store. Anyone could wear an apron. But a lab coat meant you were about to do something impor- tant. After slipping her arms through the sleeves, she felt like a real doctor. "How come you don't wear one?" she asked Mr. Tabby.

He pulled a silk handkerchief from his pants pocket and bent down to erase a smudge from the tip of his polished shoe. Then he folded the handker- chief and tucked it away. "Do I look like the sort of fellow who would wear a lab coat?"

Both Ben and Pearl shook their heads.

"Now, if you'll follow me." Mr. Tabby led the way farther down the hall and opened a door marked STAFF ROOM.

The air was cozy and warm inside. A couple of tables, some chairs, and a comfy-looking sofa filled the space, along with a television that sat in the corner.

"You may take breaks in here," Mr. Tabby said. He opened a refrigerator. "Dr. Woo has provided beverages for human children. Root beer, orange soda, chocolate milk."

"Don't you think it's weird he called us *human?*" Pearl whispered to Ben. Ben nodded. The only reason to call someone else *human*, Pearl decided, was if you were *not* human.

"There are snacks in here." Mr. Tabby opened a cupboard. "You can eat anything on the lower shelf. There are salty items. There are sweet items. Do not eat anything on the middle or top shelf. The snacks on the lower shelf are appropriate for your consumption."

"What's that?" Ben asked, pointing to a bag that was stuffed to the brim with some kind of plant.

Mr. Tabby tapped his shoe impatiently. "That bag contains ivy vines, and it sits on the middle shelf. As stated a mere moment ago, do not eat anything from the middle shelf."

A bag labeled OATS and another labeled RYE sat next to the ivy. "Why would we *want* to eat that stuff?" Pearl asked.

Mr. Tabby raised his eyebrows. "I have done my research, and I understand that human children are always hungry. Be advised that the food on the middle and top shelves are for Dr. Woo's other employees."

Who eats ivy, oats, and rye? Pearl wondered. She opened her mouth to ask that exact question when a nasal voice sounded from the wall speaker. "New patient arrival. Mr. Tabby to the Identification Room."

"Duty calls," Mr. Tabby said as he quickly closed the cupboard.

"Oh, good," Pearl said. "We get to meet a new patient. What is it?" She bounced excitedly on her toes.

Mr. Tabby pulled a small device from his vest pocket. During their last visit, he'd told Ben and Pearl that the device was a creature calculator. He punched a few keys, and the little screen lit up.

His gaze traveled across the screen. "You will not be meeting the new patient."

"Why not?" Ben asked.

"Because on the danger scale, five being the most dangerous, this creature ranks a level three. You are not yet ready for a level-three encounter."

"Danger scale?" Ben shoved his hands into his pockets. "Okay. We don't need to meet it. What else can we do?"

"Hey, wait a minute. Level three doesn't sound so bad," Pearl said.

Ben cleared his throat. "Pearl, can I talk to you for a second?"

As Mr. Tabby typed on the little keypad, Ben pulled Pearl into the room's corner and whispered in her ear. "What if the other apprentice had met a level-three creature? What if that's how she disappeared?"

Pearl folded her arms and looked into Ben's brown eyes. "Maybe the other apprentice wasn't very smart," she said, her voice hushed. "I don't know about you, but I'm incredibly smart and I can take care of myself. I'm not afraid of a level-three... anything."

"You would be wise to listen to Ben," Mr. Tabby said from across the room. "You will need further training before you are ready to meet creatures that rank above level two."

"Drat," Pearl grumbled. Then she stuck out her lower lip.

"And you would be wise to avoid this particular

creature because he doesn't like humans." Mr. Tabby tucked the calculator into his vest pocket. "However, since things don't always go as planned around here, I suppose I should tell you about our new patient, just in case you accidentally bump into one another."

Ben and Pearl held their breath in anticipation.

"The new patient is a..."

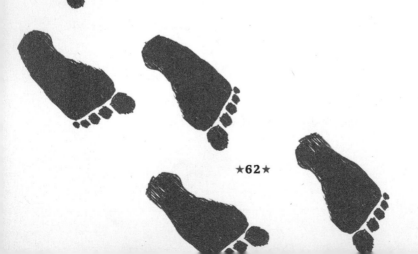

8

HE WHO HATES HUMANS

Silence fell over the Staff Room as Ben and Pearl waited to learn what sort of level-three creature did not like humans. Mr. Tabby cleared his throat. "The new patient is a leprechaun."

Pearl and Ben released their breath. "A leprechaun?" Pearl nearly laughed. She'd been expecting a three-headed dog or a giant troll. "How can a leprechaun be dangerous?"

"Isn't a leprechaun just a small person?" Ben asked.

"Never call a leprechaun *small*," Mr. Tabby said,

smoothing the front of his vest. "And never mistake a leprechaun for a human being. They are part of the fairy species, and they despise your kind."

"Why don't they like us?" Ben asked as he and Pearl followed Mr. Tabby out of the Staff Room.

"Because human beings always try to steal leprechaun gold."

"I don't want to steal gold," Pearl said. "I promise."

"I saw a movie about a leprechaun. He made shoes," Ben said.

"That is correct." Mr. Tabby nodded approvingly at Ben. "Leprechauns make the very best shoes in the Imaginary World."

"In the movie, the leprechaun could grant a wish," Ben remembered.

"A wish?" Pearl asked. "Is that true?"

Mr. Tabby sighed. "Yes. If you steal a leprechaun's gold, the leprechaun will grant a wish in exchange for the gold's return." He raised his eyebrows and leaned close. "But be warned—stealing the gold is never a good idea. Leprechauns are notorious tricksters and getting a wish granted is nearly impossible. It almost always ends badly for the human."

"Why is it here?" Ben asked as they followed Mr. Tabby farther down the hall.

"The leprechaun is male, as are all leprechauns, and fully understands human language, so please do not refer to him as *it*."

"Sorry," Ben mumbled.

"He is being treated for a head cold," Mr. Tabby said. "But enough about him. You have other duties today."

"What kind of duties?" Pearl asked. She was ready to do some work. Would she get to braid a unicorn's mane? Feed milk to a dragon hatchling? Read a story to a sick pixie?

"You will clip the sasquatch's toenails."

Ben and Pearl groaned. "We already met the sasquatch," Pearl said. The furry creature seemed nice, but it smelled horrid and had a really bad case of foot fungus. "Can't we do something else?"

"You will find the clippers in here." Mr. Tabby opened a door marked SUPPLY CLOSET. "Get the big ones. Sasquatch toenails are as thick and bristly as coconut husks."

Ben grimaced. "Can't it clip its own toenails?"

Ignoring the question, Mr. Tabby said, "You will find the sasquatch in the Forest Suite, which spans the entire third floor. Take the elevator. Do not visit any other floors. Do not leave the hospital. When you have completed the toenail task, wait for me in the lobby." His brisk steps echoed off the walls as he headed up the hall, his ponytail swishing back and forth. When he reached the exit, he called to them, "Stay out of the Identification Room, for that is where I will be examining the leprechaun." Then he stepped back into the lobby and the door closed behind him.

"This is going to be disgusting," Pearl said.

"Yeah," Ben agreed. "But at least it won't be dangerous."

The Supply Closet was crowded with all sorts of stuff like brooms, buckets, shovels, and mops. One of the walls was covered with tools. Ben found a bunch of clippers, some so small they might be used

on an insect. He grabbed the big ones. "These look like they're for hedges."

They made their way to the lobby, where the elevator doors stood open, waiting. Pearl stared longingly at the Identification Room door, which was closed. "Maybe we could just take a peek inside," she said. "I'd sure love to see what a real leprechaun looks like."

"Mr. Tabby told us to stay out of there," Ben reminded her. "This is our first day. You don't want to get into trouble on our first day, do you?"

As much as Pearl wanted to see the new patient, she didn't want to get into trouble. *Troublemaker* was her title in Buttonville. She didn't want it to be her title in Dr. Woo's hospital. "You're right." She followed Ben into the elevator. "I just thought we'd be doing something fun," she complained as she pushed button number three. "Clipping toenails doesn't sound fun at all."

"Well, maybe it will get better," Ben said.

"I sure hope so. My great-aunt Gladys asked me to clip her toenails once. They were thick and yellow. It was gross."

The doors closed, and the elevator whisked them upward. After the elevator stopped on the third floor, the doors swished open.

"Wow," Pearl said as she looked out. "Am I seeing things?"

9

THE FOREST SUITE

Although they were still inside the old button factory, Pearl and Ben stood at the edge of a living forest.

A deep layer of dirt covered the floor. Vines sprouted among gnarled roots. Trees reached to the ceiling.

Pearl took a deep breath of the warm, damp air. Beads of moisture clung to the tips of branches and glistened on fern fronds. Moss sparkled with sunlight, which streamed through a bank of windows on the far wall.

"Whoa," Ben said as a frog croaked nearby. "I want to do this to my bedroom back home. I bet our gardener would help me pick out plants."

"My parents would never let me put frogs in my room." Pearl climbed onto a big rock and stood on her tiptoes, peering over the tops of shrubs. "I don't see the sasquatch. Do you?"

"No." Ben balanced the clippers on his shoulder. "But it's brown, so it's going to blend in with the trees."

"Well, we don't blend in," Pearl said. "Our lab coats are practically glowing." Then she called, "Here, sasquatchy. Here, sasquatchy." The frogs stopped croaking, but nothing moved. She called again. Where was it hiding? "Too bad we don't have another kit."

"Yeah, too bad."

The Sasquatch Catching Kit had contained a number of helpful items—a net for trapping, a whistle for making sasquatch sounds, a tranquilizer dart for disabling, and a fog bomb to keep snoopy neighbors from witnessing the fur-covered event. The kit also held Dr. Woo's guidebook, which explained how sasquatches love sweet treats, and a chocolate bar, which Pearl had used to lead the creature through the forest.

Sweet treats? She reached into her pocket and pulled out a stick of gum. "I don't have any chocolate, but maybe this will work."

"Hey, chewing gum isn't allowed, remember?"

"Do you want to find the sasquatch or not?" She removed the wrapper, then waved the piece in the air. "Here, sasquatchy. I have something for you. It's strawberry-flavored."

A grunt sounded from across the room. Then the dirt vibrated with pounding footsteps. Tree branches swayed and shrubs rustled as the sasquatch appeared, pushing through the dense foliage. Moss and leaves clung to its matted brown fur. The scent of wet dog and sweaty socks surrounded it like a cloud. Pearl jumped off the rock and stood close to Ben. Towering over them, the creature stared at the stick of gum with its dark eyes.

"Hi," Pearl said. "Would you like this?"

"Don't ask it questions," Ben reminded her. The

guidebook had warned that sasquatches got angry when asked questions. Ben glanced down at its big, hairy feet. "I think this will be easier if we can get it to sit."

"Okay," Pearl said. She crouched next to the boulder and held the gum low to the ground. "Sit," she said.

The sasquatch scratched its sloping brow, then sat on the boulder. Pearl handed it the piece of gum. It popped the gum into its mouth, chewed, then swallowed. "No, you're not supposed to eat it," Pearl said. The scent of strawberry filled the air as the sasquatch burped.

Pearl and Ben stared at the hairy feet, which were as big as a clown's. The toenails were jagged and bristly. "Yuck," Pearl said. "You do it."

"Why me?" Ben asked.

"'Cause you have the clippers."

Ben groaned. "Fine." He knelt beside the feet. Then he pointed the clippers at one of the toes. The sasquatch whimpered.

"I'll distract it," Pearl said. "My mom always

distracts me when I have to get a shot." She opened another stick of gum and popped it into her mouth. "See," she told the creature. "Chew, chew, chew, but don't swallow."

As the sasquatch watched Pearl chew with her mouth wide open, Ben slid the clippers over a toenail. He squeezed the handles. Nothing happened. "Whoa, this toenail is as thick as wood." Gritting his teeth, he squeezed harder. *Click.* A wedge of toenail sailed through the air and ricocheted off Pearl's neck.

"Ouch," she said. "Watch it. Those things are sharp."

Ben moved the clippers to the next toenail. Gritting his teeth again, he squeezed the handles. *Click.* The toenail flew right at Ben's nose. "Ow!"

"I told you. They're like arrows."

The sasquatch growled. "Keep distracting it," Ben said.

Pearl took out another piece of gum. She chewed, then blew a bubble. The sasquatch made a soft cooing sound. "Oh, it likes that," she realized. She blew another bubble. "I'll teach you how to make bubbles." She handed the creature a second piece of gum.

As the bubble-making lesson proceeded, Ben cut another nail. He ducked as it flew over his head and impaled a tree trunk. "Who knew cutting toenails could be so dangerous? Do you think a sasquatch is a level one or a level two on the danger scale? That last toenail nearly stabbed my eyeball. Maybe we should get some safety goggles?" Then Ben's mouth fell open, and he dropped the clippers into a bed of soft moss. "Uh, speaking of eyeballs..." He pointed.

Pearl could tell from the way Ben's face had gone pale and the way his eyes had widened that something was behind her. If Ben had been smiling, she would have whipped around, eager to discover whatever cute little creature was hanging out in the Forest Suite. But his pointing hand started trembling.

Pearl froze. "What is it?" she whispered. "Ben? What are you pointing at?"

"I...I...I don't know," he stammered. "But it's... huge."

Pearl didn't like feeling afraid. The air in the Forest Suite suddenly felt cold, and goose bumps sprang up along her arms. The sasquatch didn't seem bothered, however. It had grabbed the entire pack of gum and was shoving all the pieces, including the wrappers, into its mouth.

Ever so slowly, Pearl turned around.

10

BASKETBALL EYES

Pearl looked across the landscape of ferns and trees until her gaze reached the back wall. She gasped. A large green face peered through one of the windows. Water droplets rolled down a broad snout. Tiny, round ears perched on either side of a glistening head, beside a pair of large, perfectly round eyeballs. When the eyes blinked, thick lashes brushed against the pane like feather dusters.

The Forest Suite was on the third floor, so how could something be looking at them through the

window? Maybe a giraffe with its long neck could reach that high. But giraffes were Known World creatures. And giraffes weren't green.

The eyes blinked again, and then the creature moved out of view.

Forgetting all about the sasquatch's bubble-blowing lesson, Pearl scrambled to her feet and pushed her way through the undergrowth. Sticks and pebbles crunched beneath her flip-flops. Ben followed. Then they stood side by side, their palms and faces pressed against the glass. The third floor offered a sweeping view of the lake that lay behind the old button factory. The turquoise-colored water rippled, stirred by a gentle breeze.

"Where'd it go?" Pearl's gaze darted back and forth. "Do you see it?"

"No," Ben said.

"What do you think it was?"

"I don't know, but those eyes were as big as basketballs."

"Oh, look!" A new ripple formed, larger than the others, and began to move slowly across the lake. Then a green hump emerged, followed by a tail.

"It's huge," Ben said.

With a graceful roll, the creature disappeared into the lake's depths. All that remained were some air bubbles bursting at the surface. Pearl and Ben waited, but the creature did not reappear.

"Come on," Pearl said.

"Where are you going?" Ben called as Pearl

stumbled across the mossy terrain. She leaped over a little gurgling stream.

"I want to know what that thing is."

"But we can't forget about the sasquatch," Ben said as he followed. "I've only cut three toenails."

"We'll come back and finish." She scurried around a pine tree and headed for the elevator. Its doors were closed, so Pearl pushed the down button.

"But we're not supposed to leave the hospital," Ben reminded her.

As Pearl spun around, her ponytail flicked Ben's face. "Are you serious? You want to sit up here and clip toenails? Didn't you see that thing? It was huge! It was amazing! Don't you want to get a better look?"

"Well..." Ben said, shuffling in place. "Sure, but what about the rules?"

"No one will know. We'll sneak out real quick and then come right back. Trust me, I'm good at sneaking around." Pearl punched the elevator button again.

Ben didn't say anything. He didn't have to. His clenched lips said it all.

"I know what you're thinking." Pearl set her hand gently on Ben's shoulder. "You're thinking I'm going to get you into trouble. Don't worry so much. Dr. Woo is away on an emergency, and Mr. Tabby is busy with the leprechaun. We won't get caught."

"But someone named Violet was clocked in," Ben pointed out. "Mr. Tabby said she works here, remember? What if she sees us?"

"We'll tell her that we got lost. It's our first day. We're bound to get lost on our first day." The elevator doors opened, and Pearl darted inside. "Well?" she asked. "Are you going to stay here and clip disgusting toenails, or are you going to find out what totally amazing creature is swimming in that lake?"

Ben looked over at the sasquatch. It had fallen asleep against a tree trunk, a huge wad of chewing gum stuck in its fur. "Okay," Ben said, stepping into the elevator. "I'll come with you. But I don't have a good feeling about this."

11

GREEN FACE

There was no sign of Mr. Tabby as Pearl and Ben tiptoed through the lobby. A mischievous smile spread across Pearl's face. Sneaking out of the hospital was much more exciting than clipping sasquatch toenails. She'd hoped to meet an amazing creature today. She'd hoped to have an adventure. Her dreams were about to come true.

But as soon as she unbolted and opened the front door, her smile faded. Mrs. Mulberry's car was parked just beyond the locked gate. Mrs. Mulberry sat on the hood, peering through a pair of binoculars.

Victoria Mulberry, now attired in a frilly pink dress, leaned against the car, a book propped in her hands.

"Yoo-hoo!" Mrs. Mulberry called. She slid off the hood and flung herself at the fence, her red overalls bright against the black bars. "I see you, Pearl Petal. I see you, Ben Silverstein. Let us in!"

"What are *they* doing here?" Ben asked.

"They're pests," Pearl said. "Ignore them."

"Uh, what about locking the hospital door?" Ben

asked. "Remember what happened the last time I left it unbolted?"

"Of course I remember. The sasquatch got out. But it's fast asleep upstairs, so we don't have to worry. Besides, we can't bolt it from the outside. Come on, we'll be right back."

Pearl led Ben around to the far side of the building. Unseen from the road, this section of yard had grown wild with weeds. The grass reached to Pearl's knees. As far as she could tell, it hadn't been cut since the button factory closed, so what had once been a manicured lawn had turned into a field of dandelions, daisies, and the occasional thistle. One of the thistles reached under the hem of Pearl's basketball shorts and scratched her knee, but that didn't slow her down. As she crushed the overgrowth with her flip-flops, the scents of dirt and dampness rose from the grass. Ben was close behind. He didn't move as quickly, his legs being a bit shorter than hers. Pearl was pretty sure she could beat him in a race.

"What if the creature is dangerous?" Ben asked.

"You're a total worrywart," Pearl said.

"I'm not a *total* worrywart," Ben insisted. "But I think we should go back because...because... because my grandfather told me to stay away from the lake behind the hospital. He said that once, a long time ago, some people were swimming there, and this giant whirlpool appeared, and it sucked them in. They haven't been seen since."

Pearl didn't miss a single, determined step. "Did

you just make that up?" She'd learned during their last visit that Ben liked to tell stories.

"Yeah, okay, I just made that up. But the truth is, I don't want to get eaten by whatever that thing is."

Pearl didn't want to get eaten, either, but she wanted to find out more about the green creature. "It's not going to eat us."

"You can't know that. What if it ranks a three on the danger scale? Or a four or five?"

"I'm not scared," she said.

They hurried around the corner of the building so that they were now behind the hospital. After crossing the grass, they stopped at the edge of the lake and looked into the water. Their reflections stared back at them from the surface, which was as smooth as a tabletop. Glossy lily pads floated in little clumps here and there. Except for a pair of mallard ducks, nothing appeared to be swimming above or below.

Pearl turned around. Tree branches were visible behind the third-floor windows, but the other floors were dark. "Is anyone watching us?" she asked.

"Not that I can tell," Ben replied.

"Good." Pearl ran to a rickety old dock. Some of the planks had rotted through, so she stepped carefully over those. Creaking sounds arose as she made her way to the end. Hoping to get a better view, she knelt and peered down into the water. "It's murky," she reported. "I can't see how deep it is."

Taking small, cautious steps, Ben soon joined her. "Do you think it lives on that island?" he asked, pointing. A small, pine-tree-covered island sat in the middle of the lake. A sandy beach ran around the island's perimeter.

"Maybe," Pearl said, getting to her feet. Cocking her head, she listened but heard nothing unusual—just a few twittering birds. Then she took a deep breath, cupped her hands around her mouth, and hollered, "Hey! Green creature! Where are you?"

Ben gasped. "What are you doing?" He looked back over his shoulder. "If you yell like that, someone at the hospital will hear you."

"I want the *creature* to hear me," Pearl said. She was about to call out again when a ripple appeared at the far end of the lake, disturbing a patch of lily pads.

"Uh-oh." Ben took a step back as a green head emerged. The head was attached to a neck that gradually rose from the water, higher and higher and higher, until the head hovered far above the lake. Pearl and Ben gawked, their mouths wide open. It was a moment of pure wonder.

"It looks like a sea monster," Ben whispered.

"A sea monster," Pearl whispered back. "An actual sea…" She frowned. "But it's living in a lake."

"Maybe it's a lake monster. Like the Loch Ness monster."

"The Loch Ness monster?" Pearl kept her voice low. Yelling had been a fine thing to do when she'd been trying to get the creature's attention, but now that she was face-to-face with its enormity, she thought it best to be as quiet as possible. She leaned close to Ben, aiming her hushed voice at his ear. "Do you think this creature is related to the Loch Ness monster?"

Ben shrugged. "I don't know. I thought the Loch

Ness monster was a hoax. I thought all those photos were fakes."

Pearl knew exactly what he was talking about. There was a book called *Terrifying Secrets of Loch Ness* at the Buttonville Bookstore. Before she'd been banned from the store, Pearl had spent many a morning there, tucked into the far corner, reading whatever suited her mood. The book was filled with photos of a monster that supposedly inhabited Loch Ness, a lake in Scotland. The pictures were always grainy, mostly shot in black and white, of a long-necked creature that looked a bit like a dinosaur. None of the photos offered a close-up view or any details like facial expressions or skin texture. She'd concluded that the sightings were hoaxes. "Well, *this* lake monster is totally real," she whispered.

Stretching its neck, the creature ripped pine needles from the top of a tree. Water dripped off its snout as it munched, its jaw moving leisurely like a cow chewing cud. When it swallowed, a big, roundish lump traveled down the length of its

neck in slow motion. "Cool!" Ben said with a burst of enthusiasm.

Alerted by Ben's exclamation, the lake monster turned and looked toward the dock. It stopped chewing, narrowing its round eyes. "Oh no," Ben said. "It's coming this way." He took a few steps backward.

Pearl wasn't sure how to react. Part of her wanted to retreat to a safer distance, but the other part of her couldn't believe her luck. Compared with this amazing creature, the sasquatch seemed so... ordinary. She slowly raised her hand and waved as the lake monster glided through the water, getting closer and closer.

And closer.

"Wow, it's really big," Pearl realized. "Really, really big." She took a couple of steps backward, just to be on the safe side. "Do you think it's as big as a dinosaur?"

Ben appeared to be frozen with fear because his feet weren't moving, nor was any part of his face. He stared up as the monster towered over the dock.

Green scales, each glistening with droplets of water, covered its face and neck. It lowered its head until it was eye level with Pearl. Then they stared at each other.

Pearl found it hard to breathe, not because the creature smelled fishy but because she was laughing, gasping, and squealing at the same time. Was this truly happening? Was she face-to-face with a creature as big as a brontosaurus? Or was she dreaming?

The monster snorted, spraying Pearl's face with flecks of goo. *Yep, I'm wide awake,* she told herself, wiping her face with her lab coat sleeve. The basketball-sized eyes blinked at her. They contained every color of green Pearl had ever seen, from Robin Hood green to four-leaf-clover green to lime-sherbet green. The lashes were jet black and curled at the ends. Pearl's reflection stared back at her from the creature's irises. "You're beautiful," Pearl said.

It flared its nostrils and sniffed the top of Pearl's head.

Pearl wasn't sure what to do. Should she run?

Should she call for help? Nothing this large had ever smelled her hair. Maybe Ben was right. Maybe they should have stayed in the Forest Suite, clipping toenails. Being jabbed by a flying toenail was a lot less dangerous than standing mere inches away from a real, living, breathing lake monster. The monster bent its neck and sniffed Pearl's toes. Then, with a graceful lunge, it reached past Pearl and grabbed some grass from the lake's edge. It chewed the blades contentedly, its eyes half closed.

Everything was okay. No one was hurt. No one was in trouble.

Pearl and Ben sighed with relief, their shoulders relaxing. "That was freaky," Ben said. "I thought it was going to eat you."

"Me, too," Pearl admitted. Then, ever so slowly, she reached out and patted the creature's neck. "The scales feel soft and slippery. Do you think it's a girl or a boy?"

"I don't know," Ben said with a shrug. Cautiously, he reached out and touched the scales. "They're kinda slimy."

The creature kept chewing and didn't seem to mind one bit that two humans were petting it. "Aren't you glad we did this?" Pearl asked. "How many kids get to pet a lake monster?"

Ben smiled. "Yeah, it's pretty cool."

The monster swallowed, then turned and sniffed the top of Ben's head. Ben froze again as hot breath blew through his hair. "It tickles," he mumbled. The monster sniffed Ben's lab coat, then his brand-new sneakers, which were now covered in grass stains.

"I told you we wouldn't get into trouble," Pearl said with a little laugh. It was funny to watch the creature nudge Ben with its big snout. "Sometimes it's okay to break the rules."

And that's when the lake monster wrapped its mouth around Ben's middle and picked him up.

Right into the air!

12

Stop!" Pearl ordered, but the creature didn't obey.

Ben kicked his legs. "Put me down!" he hollered, pounding the green snout with his fists.

"Jump," Pearl called. "Jump into the water."

"I can't jump. It won't let me go!" He pounded some more. "Help! Help!"

Pearl shielded her eyes from the sun, watching helplessly as Ben rose higher and higher into the air. How do you stop a lake monster—or any monster, for that matter—from taking your friend?

This was a terrible turn of events. Ben was going to get eaten, and it was all her fault. He'd wanted to stay inside the hospital. He'd wanted to finish clipping the sasquatch's toenails. But she'd insisted that they go outside. "Hey!" she screamed with all her might. "You bring him back! Bring him back right now!"

Ben got smaller and smaller as the monster straightened its neck. Dangling far above the water, Ben stopped struggling and peered down at Pearl, his eyes wide with fear. Then, as quickly as it had scooped him up, the creature set Ben on the little island. It proceeded to rip some pine needles from a tree and returned to chewing as if deep in thought.

The island wasn't that far away. Pearl guessed she could swim to its beach in only a few minutes. "Ben," she called from the end of the dock. "Can you hear me?"

"Yes!" he answered as he scrambled to his feet. He hurried to the edge of the beach. "How am I going to get off this island?" His voice carried easily across the water.

"Maybe the lake monster will bring you back," she suggested hopefully, though the creature seemed to have forgotten all about Ben.

"No way," Ben said, shaking his head violently. "I'm not doing that again."

Pearl looked around. No one seemed to have noticed the commotion. There was a possibility that they still might not get into trouble. "Swim," she said, mimicking a swimmer's stroke. "Hurry!"

"Swim?" Ben looked down at his lab coat and jeans, as if worried about ruining them. "I think you should go get Mr. Tabby. He might have a boat or something like that."

"If I go and get Mr. Tabby, then we'll be fired for sure." Pearl stomped her foot. "Come on, you can do it. Swim!"

Ben appeared to have accepted Pearl's logic because he took off his shoes, tied the laces together, and slung them over his shoulder. He tucked his socks into his pants pockets and stepped into the shallows. The lake monster stopped chewing. As Ben waded up to his ankles, the monster cocked its head.

"It's cold," Ben announced. "Really, really cold."

"Hurry!"

His teeth gritted, Ben waded deeper into the glistening water. And deeper...

The lake monster grabbed him around the waist and plopped him back onto the island's beach.

Ben was quick to respond. Like a boxer, he leaped to his feet. Then he ducked beneath the monster's neck and stumbled into the water. Splashing, he'd made it up to his knees before the monster grabbed him again and deposited him in the sand.

They repeated this two more times. The monster smiled as if playing a game of fetch. But Ben didn't smile. He waved his fist and stared into the basketball-sized eyes. "Let me go!"

After one more unsuccessful escape attempt, Ben sank to the sand and sat, his shoulders hunched with defeat. "What am I supposed to do now?" he called.

"I don't know," Pearl admitted, having never been in this particular situation. She'd watched the goings-on with a mixture of fascination and horror. Getting away was clearly not going to be easy.

The lake monster grinned, revealing a row of pointy, green-stained teeth. Then it tore some needles from a tree and set them at Ben's feet. The monster nudged the needles closer, offering to share. It nudged and nudged until Ben grabbed a handful of needles and pretended to eat. The monster nodded. Was it going to keep Ben the way a kid might keep a frog or a hamster?

Maybe it *was* time to get some help. "I'll be right back," she hollered. Then she ran up the creaky dock as fast as she could.

A thistle scraped Pearl's ankle as she hurried around the building, but the scratch didn't hurt half as much as the worry that was knotting her stomach. Now Ben would be added to the long list of people who thought of her as a troublemaker. How come no one ever talked about the good things she'd done for the town—like the time she picked up the litter along the highway, or the time she sold lemonade and gave the money to the Buttonville Senior Center? How come people only remembered the bad things—like the time she tried to make a pond behind the Dollar Store and it flooded the street, or the time she climbed onto the roof of the hardware store to collect a bird nest and one of the roof tiles fell off and dented Mr. Wanamaker's new outdoor grill?

But this event would be the worst one of all. This would be the one they'd talk about forever— the day Pearl Petal took that nice Ben Silverstein down to the lake, against the rules, and he got kidnapped by a giant green monster.

She raced around the corner and up to the hospital's front door.

"Yoo-hoo!" Mrs. Mulberry called from outside the gate. "I see you, Pearl Petal. Let us in!"

Without a word or a glance at Mrs. Mulberry, Pearl rushed inside. Then she closed and bolted the door behind her. As she stood in the empty lobby, her frantic breathing echoed off the walls. What should she do? *What should she do?*

This time, the door to the Identification Room stood open. No one was inside. Where had Mr. Tabby gone? Surely he could help, but then he'd know that Pearl had broken the rules. And he would probably tell Dr. Woo, and Dr. Woo would probably fire her. Pearl didn't want to lose the apprenticeship. The chance to work with Imaginary creatures was the best thing that had ever happened in her entire life. Could she figure out a way to rescue Ben without Mr. Tabby's help?

But nothing came to mind. Not a darn thing.

Pearl groaned. Dr. Woo might return from her emergency visit at any moment and find Ben stuck on that island. Time was wasting. If only Pearl could wish this all away.

Wish it all away?

She grinned. Why, of course.

Somewhere in Dr. Woo's hospital for Imaginary creatures, there was a new patient who could grant wishes.

13

This was the second time Pearl had been inside the Identification Room. During the first visit, Mr. Tabby had examined the dragon hatchling. Then he'd set the wounded creature onto a conveyor belt, which had carried the hatchling away to surgery.

The wide belt ran from an examination table and through a large hole in the wall. Had Mr. Tabby put the leprechaun on the conveyor belt? It made sense. Pearl peered into the hole. It was dark in there. She reached her hand inside and felt the sides of a tunnel but nothing more.

So she climbed onto the belt and sat with her legs crisscrossed. After tucking the hem of her lab coat under her bottom so it wouldn't get caught on anything, she pushed the conveyor belt's button. A humming sound arose, like a trapped housefly, and the belt began to move. For a brief moment, Pearl second-guessed herself and almost jumped off. But then what would she do? The leprechaun seemed the best way to fix things without Mr. Tabby or Dr. Woo finding out.

As Pearl entered the tunnel, she ducked her head and wrapped her arms around her knees. She remembered the Tunnel of Love ride she'd taken at the Milkydale County Fair last summer. But instead of sitting on a conveyor belt, she'd sat in a little heart-shaped boat.

It was dark inside the tunnel. And cold. The belt moved slowly, deeper into the blackness, then took a turn to the right, then a turn to the left. A

few moments later, rays of light greeted her as she emerged into another room.

This room had nothing in it except for a chalkboard, upon which someone had written in white chalk:

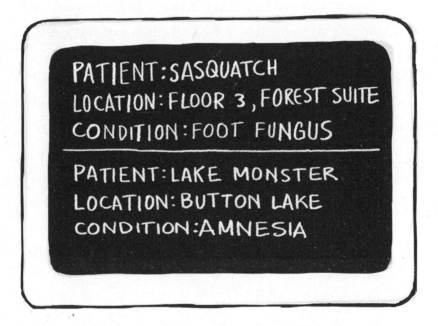

PATIENT: SASQUATCH
LOCATION: FLOOR 3, FOREST SUITE
CONDITION: FOOT FUNGUS

PATIENT: LAKE MONSTER
LOCATION: BUTTON LAKE
CONDITION: AMNESIA

Amnesia? Pearl thought. She'd heard the term before. A person who has amnesia is unable to remember things, like who he is or where he'd come from. But she'd never heard of an animal having amnesia.

Then she found what she was looking for.

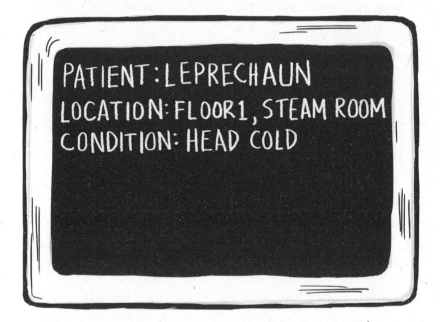

PATIENT: LEPRECHAUN
LOCATION: FLOOR 1, STEAM ROOM
CONDITION: HEAD COLD

Pearl figured that because the conveyor belt hadn't traveled uphill, she was still on the first floor. After scooting off the belt, she opened the door and peered into a hallway. Directly across was a door labeled OINTMENT ROOM. The next door was labeled

PARASITE REMOVAL ROOM. The Steam Room was the third door down. As she tiptoed up to it, she tried to remember exactly what Mr. Tabby had said. *If you take a leprechaun's gold, he will grant you a wish.* How difficult could it be? Leprechauns were small, so they couldn't put up a very big fight...could they? Slowly, she cracked open the Steam Room door and peeked in.

A very small figure sat on top of a table. He was about the size of the garden gnome statues that Mrs. Froot, the oldest person in Buttonville, kept all over her front yard. His leather apron overflowed with tools of all shapes and sizes, his white shirtsleeves were rolled up, and his black hair was tied back in a knot. A humidifier hummed in the corner, spraying menthol-scented steam into the air.

Wow, Pearl thought. *It's a real, living, breathing leprechaun. A very small person.* Then she remembered that he wasn't a person after all—he was a fairy.

"Brrrt." He blew his nose into a tissue, then

wadded the tissue and dropped it onto the floor, where it joined dozens of others. Pearl caught a quick glimpse of his profile as he grabbed another tissue. His nose was red and glistening. "Cobblestone be all snuffly," he grumbled. "Sniffly and snuffly."

Pearl took a quick breath. There it was, a rusty coffee can right next to the leprechaun. Something shimmered from within.

Gold.

Pearl dashed into the room. "Ugh," she groaned as she snatched the can, which was surprisingly heavy. The coins clinked, and glimmering dust rose into the air. The leprechaun spun around, his eyes wide with surprise.

"Cobblestone's gold," he said, pointing to the can. His face turned as red as his swollen nose. "Why do you steal from Cobblestone?"

"I'm not stealing," Pearl said. "I'm...*borrowing.*"

"Then return it to Cobblestone." He got to his feet. Gold dust speckled his black beard and black boots.

Pearl was confused. "Is *your* name Cobblestone,

or are you talking about someone else?"

"Cobblestone stands before you." He held out his arms. "Now give Cobblestone his treasure."

Pearl stepped away, hugging the can to her chest. It was as heavy as an armful of bricks. She wasn't sure how long she could hold it. "I'll give it back if you grant me a wish."

The leprechaun sneezed. A little cloud of golden dust shot out of his nose. "What be the name of the thief who steals from Cobblestone?"

Pearl didn't like being called a thief, but she *was* holding something that didn't belong to her. "My name is Pearl."

"Pearl?" He furrowed his brow. "Pearl be a fairy name. You be a strange-looking fairy. Where be your wings?"

"I'm not a fairy," Pearl said. "I'm just a regular girl."

"Human?" The word hissed out. "Cobblestone doesn't like humans."

"You like Dr. Woo, don't you? She's a human."

"Dr. Woo never tries to steal from Cobblestone."

"I only did it because you're supposed to grant me a wish if I get your gold." One wish would take care of everything. Pearl chewed on her lower lip as she noticed the tools hanging from the leprechaun's apron. Some looked supersharp. What if he got mad and tried to poke her? He was a level three on the danger scale, after all, and not fond of human beings. "My friend is in trouble, and I need a wish so I can set him free."

"Cobblestone has no wishes. His magic be clogged with sniffles and snot." He blew his nose into a tissue.

Pearl remembered Mr. Tabby's warning: *Leprechauns are notorious tricksters and getting a wish granted is nearly impossible. It almost always ends badly for the human.* Was the leprechaun lying about his magic? Was he trying to trick her? "Then I guess you don't want your gold. I'll just be leaving. There's a nice bank in town where I can deposit it." She lifted her foot, preparing to take a step.

"Wait." He rubbed his red nose. "Cobblestone has no magic. But Cobblestone will trade with you instead." He pointed to her feet. "Your human shoes be hideous. Cobblestone will make you a pair of leprechaun shoes if you return his gold."

A pair of leprechaun shoes?

The little guy smiled sweetly. "Would Pearl the regular girl like a pair of dancing shoes made from lightning-bug wings or a pair of running shoes made from the wind? How about a pair of slippers made from spun clouds?"

Spun clouds? Nothing in the Dollar Store was made from spun clouds.

"Cobblestone be the best cobbler in all the Imaginary World. He can make shoes from anything." He puffed out his chest. "You will be the envy of your friends."

Her friends? Pearl looked away for a moment. She'd gotten her only friend trapped on an island with a lake monster, and now she was thinking about shoes? "I don't need new shoes." She rattled the can. "I need a wish. Are you going to grant me a wish, or am I going to use this gold to buy myself a chewing-gum factory?"

He folded his arms. "What be your wish?"

Pearl smiled with satisfaction. Now they were getting somewhere. "My friend, Ben, is stuck on an island because a lake monster took him and won't let him go. I want you to grant me a wish to get Ben off the island without Dr. Woo or Mr. Tabby or anyone else finding out."

"A lake monster, you say?" He sneezed, and this time the gold dust shot out of his ears. "Lake monsters have tiny fish brains. They be easy to trick. Take Cobblestone to the lake monster."

Pearl knew it was wrong to take an Imaginary creature out of the hospital. When the sasquatch had escaped, Mr. Tabby had said that Imaginary creatures were not allowed in the Known World. But the lake monster was living in the lake, so it must be safe out there on the hospital grounds. Pearl simply had to keep the leprechaun from going beyond the wrought-iron fence and into the town of Buttonville. If a leprechaun was spotted running around, magazine and television reporters would show up and Dr. Woo's hospital for Imaginary creatures would be discovered, no doubt about it.

"You must follow me," she told him with a stern look. "Don't go anywhere else."

He nodded.

Everything will be okay, Pearl told herself as she walked back up the hall, the gold's weight making her footsteps wobbly. A wish would be granted, a boy set free. She didn't have to turn around to know the leprechaun was following, because his high-heeled boots made little clacking sounds.

After they'd both climbed onto the conveyor belt, Pearl pushed the button. The belt hummed and began its return journey. Pearl ducked her head as she entered the dark tunnel.

There was still no sign of Mr. Tabby as Pearl and

Cobblestone made their way from the Identification Room and through the lobby. Pearl unbolted and opened the hospital's front door. Unfortunately, Mrs. Mulberry and Victoria were still waiting behind the gates. Were they going to sit there all day? Didn't they have anything better to do? The leprechaun peeked around Pearl's knee. "Humans," he grumbled as he spied the pair. "Cobblestone doesn't like humans."

"There are good humans and bad humans," Pearl said. "And those are definitely *bad* humans." How could she sneak the leprechaun past the Mulberrys? "Stay behind me," she told him. Then, like a crab, she walked sideways along the front of the building, shielding the leprechaun from view. Victoria never looked up from her book, but Mrs. Mulberry continued to spy through her binoculars.

"Yoo-hoo! I see you, Pearl Petal. And I see..." Mrs. Mulberry fell silent.

Pearl moved as quickly as she could. Once they'd turned the corner and were out of sight, she led the way down the path that she and Ben had trampled earlier. The leprechaun's tools clanked and clinked as he followed. "Perhaps you want a pair of princess shoes made from dwarf crystals. They sparkle and be pink."

"Princess shoes?" She rolled her eyes. "Why would I want sparkly pink princess shoes?"

"She who wears princess shoes be destined to meet a prince."

"A prince?" The gold's weight pulled on Pearl's arms. "A *real* prince?" There were no princes in Buttonville, unless you counted Harvey Dill, who'd been crowned Prince of Buttons in last year's Founders Day parade. He got to wear a button-covered cloak and a plastic crown from the Dollar Store.

"Of course a real prince. Results be guaranteed in seventy-two hours."

"Hold on a minute." Pearl stopped walking and looked down at the leprechaun. "Are you saying that if I wear a pair of shoes called princess shoes, I will meet a real prince in..." She counted the hours in her head. "In three days?" He nodded.

While Pearl had no desire to wear sparkly shoes, the result sounded interesting. Would the prince arrive in Buttonville on a horse? Would he fly in on a private jet? Maybe he'd spend a lot of money at the Dollar Store. That would be great.

"Never mind rescuing the boy named Ben." The leprechaun held out his hands. "Give Cobblestone the gold and you will have a pair of princess shoes."

A breeze blew across Pearl's face. She imagined a front-page photo in the *Buttonville Gazette* of her and Prince Whatever-His-Name-Was. This time the headline wouldn't be about her troublemaking. "Well..." She wiggled her toes against the Dollar Store flip-flops. "Well..."

"Help!" Ben's voice shot through the air.

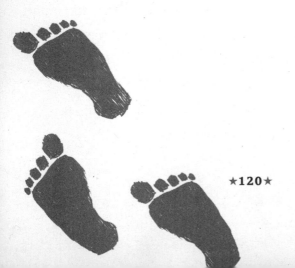

14

As far as Pearl could tell, things weren't going well over on the island. The lake monster was licking the side of Ben's face the way a momma cat would lick her kitten.

Poor Ben, Pearl thought.

Then the monster stuck its green head into the lake and emerged with a wiggling fish in its mouth. After dropping the fish next to Ben, it blinked its huge eyes expectantly. Ben picked up the fish and pretended to take a bite. The monster smiled and licked Ben's face again.

"There he is," Pearl told the leprechaun as they stood at the end of the dock. "I need you to get him off that island. As soon as you do that, you can have your gold." Then she called, "Hi, Ben!"

Ben looked across the narrow expanse of water that separated the dock and the island. He dropped the fish and stared, openmouthed, at Cobblestone. Pearl could guess what he was thinking: *Oh no, what has she done* now?

"Don't worry! He's a leprechaun. He's going to grant me a wish. I have his gold."

"Are you crazy?" Ben shouted. Another lick from the creature toppled him onto the sand. He wiped his face with his sleeve. Pearl wondered if they had any shampoo at the Dollar Store that would wash away lake-monster slobber.

"Go ahead," she urged the leprechaun. "Do your magic."

"Cobblestone told you he has no magic. Why do you not believe?"

She didn't want to call him a trickster to his face. "There's no time to argue about this. Just help me. Please."

He shrugged. "Cobblestone thinks you should leave the human boy on the island. He be fine."

"Leave him on the island? I can't do that."

"Why not?"

She frowned. "Because he doesn't have a sleeping bag or a toothbrush. And he can't eat raw fish and pine needles. And if he doesn't go home this afternoon, his grandfather will come looking for him. Then the police will come looking. And if they find out about this hospital, Dr. Woo will have to move again, and I don't want her to move. I want to keep working here."

She couldn't hold the coffee can any longer. With a grunt, she dropped it between her feet. As she did, the can's rusty rim fell off. "Sorry," she said, trying to put the piece back into place. The leprechaun glowered at her. "I said I was sorry. Why do you keep your gold in this cruddy old can anyway?"

His eyes drooped with sadness. "The last human who stole Cobblestone's gold also stole Cobblestone's beautiful pot."

"Oh." Pearl felt a bit sorry for the little guy. And even though the situation with Ben was urgent, questions popped into her mind. Pearl had never

★124★

been good at holding back questions. "Did your beautiful pot get stolen in the Known World? Or did it get stolen in the Imaginary World, and if so, does that mean that there are humans living in the Imaginary World?"

He looked away and mumbled something under his breath. Then he turned his back to her.

She sighed. "Look," she said. "I'm sorry that I've ruined your rusty coffee can. And I'm sorry that I took your gold, but it was the only way I could get you to help me. Could you please use your magic and get Ben off the island? Then you can go back to the Steam Room, and I can get back to being an apprentice."

"Achooo!" Gold dust sprayed from his inflamed nostrils. "Cobblestone told you. Cobblestone's magic be clogged with sniffles and snot. That's why Cobblestone came to see Dr. Woo. When Cobblestone be cured, Cobblestone's magic will return."

Pearl stomped her foot. "You're still trying to trick me." Mustering her bossiest voice, she pointed

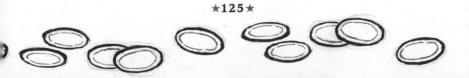

at him. "You'd better grant me my wish or—"

The dock shook as something large and green crashed into one of the posts. Pearl jumped back. The lake monster's long neck arched, then sprang at its target. "Aaaah!" cried the leprechaun as he rose into the air, plucked from the dock as if he were a ripe berry.

Oh no! This was going all wrong. Pearl stood helplessly, her arms hanging limp at her sides, watching as the leprechaun was carried to the island. With a plunk, he landed in the sand. Ben, who'd taken the opportunity to try swimming again, was yanked from the shallows and deposited next to the leprechaun. They looked at each other. Then they turned and glared across the water at Pearl. The lake monster dumped a fish right on the leprechaun's lap and smiled.

Pearl stomped her foot. *Drat a million times!*

But, hey, maybe this wasn't such a terrible turn of events. Surely the leprechaun would use his magic to get himself off the island. And he could bring Ben with him. "Cobblestone," she called, pointing to the coffee can. "I still have your gold. Bring Ben and you can have it."

Cobblestone tossed the fish aside and sneezed, then sneezed again. He folded his arms and remained sitting in the sand. Why wasn't he doing anything? Did he truly have no magic? His next sneeze was so loud, it echoed off the hospital's back wall.

Ben knelt next to the leprechaun and said something to him. Then he called out to Pearl. "I think he's got a fever. He's all sweaty."

Fever? A shudder ran up Pearl's spine. A fever came when someone was really sick.

Ben ducked as the monster tried to lick his face again. "Pearl," he yelled. "Go! Get! Mister! Tabby!"

He was right. She hated to admit it, but her plan was a disaster. What if the leprechaun got sicker? What if he got so sick that he...?

She needed help.

She ran up the dock and was about to jump off when she noticed a signpost that had fallen over. Pushing the green blades aside, she read the sign's message.

Lonely?

A knot formed in Pearl's gut. She didn't like that word. It had been a rough couple of years in Buttonville since most of the kids and their families had moved away. Even though she'd tried to keep herself busy with adventures, playing alone was a drag. Loneliness had become a common feeling for Pearl, as common as the ache of an empty stomach in the morning. But now it made sense. The creature had taken Ben and the leprechaun because it wanted friends.

A shadow fell over Pearl's face, and she darted away before the lake monster's jaws snapped shut. The creature had sneaked up on her. Its long neck reached the length of the dock. "You're not taking me to your island," Pearl told it. It batted its lashes innocently. Then it made a soft sighing sound. Pearl craned her neck, looking up at the huge green face. Was that a tear sparkling in the corner of its eye or just lake water? "I'm sorry you're lonely," she said, softening her voice. The creature cocked its head, listening. "I wish I could find you some

friends, but I don't know any other lake monsters."
If the creature had some friends, it might let Ben
and the leprechaun go.

And then, a plan as brilliant as the sun filled
Pearl's mind.

Maybe the friends didn't have to be *real* lake
monsters.

"I'll be right back."

15

THE THING
IN AISLE FIVE

Pearl was determined to make everything right, all by herself.

Once she reached the front of the hospital, she started across the lawn, then stopped dead in her tracks. A police car was parked on the road next to Mrs. Mulberry's car.

"Aunt Milly," Pearl grumbled as she crouched, out of sight, in the tall grasses.

Aunt Milly, known as Officer Milly to the residents of Buttonville, worked the day shift for the Buttonville Police Force. She was standing next to the squad car, her thumbs hooked in her belt loops, her navy shirt neatly tucked into her navy pants. Sunlight gleamed along the polished rims of her dark glasses. Mrs. Mulberry was talking to Officer Milly. Pearl couldn't hear what she was saying, but she was waving her arms around in frantic gestures. Victoria Mulberry sat on the sidewalk reading her book, paying no attention to her busybody mother.

Moving on all fours, as slyly as a tiger, Pearl made her way across the field. The last thing she wanted was to talk to her aunt *and* the Mulberrys, so she headed toward a distant section of the wrought-iron fence. The fence had been designed with sharp points at the top, which made it dangerous to climb over. During their first visit, when they'd brought the dragon hatchling, Pearl and Ben had climbed over the front gate, which didn't have sharp points. But with Aunt Milly and the Mulberrys in the way, the gate was not an option.

Luckily, on one of her adventuring days, Pearl had discovered a narrow fence segment where the points had rusted away. The area was partially camouflaged by a cluster of trees. After tossing her flip-flops to the other side, she pulled herself up and over, then landed on the sidewalk. Darting behind a tree, Pearl quieted her breath and listened. Although her aunt Milly and Mrs. Mulberry stood many yards away, the breeze carried the conversation right to Pearl's ears.

"Let me get this straight," Officer Milly said. "You called the police department to report an emergency, and the emergency is that you saw a small person."

"It was a *very* small person," Mrs. Mulberry said.

"You saw a child?"

"No, not a child. For goodness' sake, how could he be a child? He had a beard. He was *very* small and *very* bearded."

Officer Milly cleared her throat. "There are no laws against being small."

"But who is he? That's what I want to know. I'm the president of the Buttonville Welcome Wagon. It's my job to know if someone new comes to Buttonville."

"Maybe he's a friend of Dr. Woo's," Officer Milly said.

"But he was with your niece, Pearl Petal."

"Pearl is working for Dr. Woo. So is Ben Silverstein."

"And why is that?" asked Mrs. Mulberry. "Pearl is a known troublemaker, and Ben just moved here. Why didn't Dr. Woo hire my daughter? Victoria is a straight-A student and never gets into trouble."

"I don't want to work for Dr. Woo," Victoria complained. "I don't like worms."

"Be quiet, dear, and read your book," Mrs. Mulberry said. Then her voice grew louder and more insistent. "Officer Milly, your job is to help the residents of Buttonville, and we need your help. This entire situation is very mysterious and sneaky. The gate is locked, and we can't get in. I want you to order Dr. Woo to open this gate."

"There are no laws against locking gates on private property," Officer Milly pointed out.

"But I am the president of the Welcome Wagon!"

Pearl didn't have time to listen to this nonsense. After slipping back into her flip-flops, she hurried across the road, glancing over her shoulder to make certain she hadn't been spotted. Mrs. Mulberry and her aunt Milly were still talking. Victoria was still reading. As fast as she could, Pearl ran to town, wishing all the while that she were wearing a pair of leprechaun running shoes made from the wind.

How many rules had she broken today? She'd lost count.

After charging through the Dollar Store door, she bumped right into her mother. "What's the matter?" Mrs. Petal asked, grabbing hold of Pearl's shoulders. "Are you okay?"

"Yeah, I'm okay." Pearl wiped beads of sweat from the back of her neck.

"Why are you out of breath? And why is your face red?" But before she could ask more questions, a bell rang. Mr. Bumfrickle, a retired button-factory worker, was waiting at the checkout counter with a basket of shoe polish and greeting cards. Mrs. Petal leaned close to her daughter and whispered, "You're not in trouble, are you?"

"No," Pearl replied honestly, because she wasn't in trouble—not yet. And she wouldn't be if she got back to the hospital before Mr. Tabby noticed that the leprechaun was missing.

Mrs. Petal smiled with relief and kissed Pearl's cheek. Then she began to ring up Mr. Bumfrickle's items on the register.

Pearl had come to the Dollar Store to collect two things. She hurried past Lemon Face, who clung to his perch, singing to his reflection. At the top of the stairs, she veered left and into her bedroom, where she grabbed the Pot O'Gold game from the shelf. After tucking the Sasquatch Catching certificate inside a different game, Pearl dumped the plastic leprechauns, rainbows, and gold pieces onto the carpet—she'd clean them up later. Empty pot in hand, she hurried back downstairs.

The second thing she'd come to get was in the beauty-supply section of aisle five, where Pearl's

father was straightening shampoo bottles. "Say, that's a nice lab coat," he said. "You look very official."

"Thanks."

He looked at his watch. "Aren't you supposed to be at the worm hospital until three o'clock?"

"I'm taking a break."

"Where's Ben?"

"He's back at the hospital doing...worm stuff."

Mr. Petal scratched his blond head. "Worm stuff? What kind of worm stuff?"

Pearl's entire body tensed. "Uh...he's feeding them. It's lunchtime." She scanned the shelves. Toothbrushes, shower caps, loofahs, nail files...Aha! Mirrors.

"Worms have lunchtime?" Mr. Petal laughed. "What do they eat?"

"Worm food." Pearl grabbed the biggest mirror, a round one with a pink frame. "Can I have this? It's for the hospital."

"For the worms?" Mr. Petal raised his eyebrows. "Why would a worm need a mirror?"

Pearl cringed. If there was a moment when she

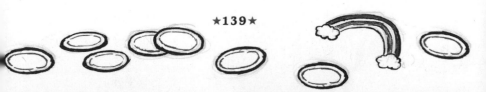

needed Ben, it was this moment. He knew how to come up with the best stories.

"Uh…uh…" she stammered, her thoughts racing. Would a worm want to look at its own reflection? Do worms have eyes? They live in the dark. Maybe they don't have eyes. Pearl realized she didn't know the first thing about worms. She chewed on her lower lip. "Uh…uh…" And wouldn't a mirror be dangerous to a worm? Mirrors reflect sunlight. If a mirror reflected the sun onto a worm, the worm would get all dried up. Isn't a dried-up worm a dead worm? "It's not for the worms," she said. "It's actually for Dr. Woo. She's very pretty. I wanted to give her a thank-you present for letting me work at her hospital."

Mr. Petal nodded. "That's very considerate." Over in his cage, Lemon Face twittered as if in agreement.

"I'm wondering, now that there's a worm hospital in Buttonville, maybe we should start carrying worm food in the store."

"Good idea," Pearl called as she hurried up the aisle. "See ya at three o'clock."

Then, success nearly at hand, she ran around Mr. Bumfrickle and out the Dollar Store door.

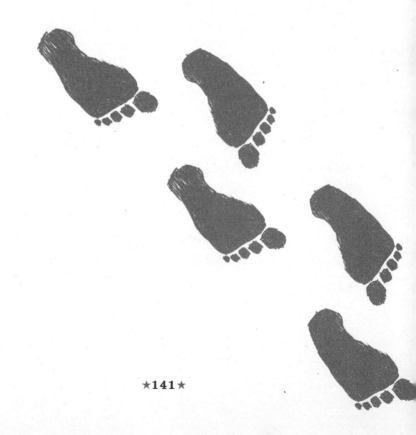

16

TWO SHINY GIFTS

When Pearl arrived back at the old button factory, she sighed with relief. The Mulberrys and her aunt Milly were gone. *Phew!* That made things a lot easier. But it was probably best not to climb over the gate in full view, just in case someone came driving past. So, after crossing the street, she ran toward the cluster of shady trees that hid the rusted section of fence, then skidded to a stop.

A very pink, very frilly Victoria Mulberry stepped out from behind a tree. "Hello, *Pearl*." She said the word *Pearl* as if it tasted like cod-liver oil.

Pearl narrowed her eyes. "Hello, *Victoria*." She said the word *Victoria* as if it tasted like boiled brussels sprouts, which it did. "Where's your mother?"

"She went to get sandwiches. Spying on people makes her super hungry." Victoria tucked her book under her arm, then slid her glasses up her nose. "Whatcha doing with that golden pot and that mirror?"

"None of your beeswax," Pearl said. How was she going to climb over the fence without revealing the secret climbing spot? She had to get rid of Victoria. "If you want an appointment to see the doctor, you need to have a worm."

Victoria sneered. "I don't have a worm, *Pearl*."

"Then you should find one, *Victoria*."

The sneer rose higher. Turned out, Victoria's upper lip had gotten caught on her blue braces. She pulled it free, then said, "I don't know where to find a worm."

Pearl looked around, then stepped closer to Victoria, as if she were about to reveal a big secret.

"Dr. Woo told me that on nice summer days, worms like to go swimming. They take their families to the park and float in the water." Pearl nearly laughed. Ben would be so impressed by her crazy story.

Victoria narrowed her eyes. "Dr. Woo said that?" Pearl nodded. "Well, guess what? I already knew worms like to go swimming." After a persnickety "*humph*," Victoria hurried away, her frizzy red hair and pink ruffled dress bouncing with each step.

Pearl didn't waste another second. After sliding the mirror and flip-flops through the bars and tossing the plastic pot over the fence, she climbed quickly, landing on the other side with a victorious smile. Then she ran to the lake.

Ben and the leprechaun were still sitting on the island's beach, a growing pile of fish between them. While the lake monster pulled reeds from the shallows and chewed, watching its captives with a satisfied smile, Pearl went over her plan in her head.

The goal was to get Ben and the leprechaun off the island. The leprechaun had said that lake monsters have tiny brains. Lemon Face, Pearl's parakeet, also had a tiny brain. Pearl figured that if a tiny-brained bird thought his reflection was a friend, a tiny-brained lake monster might think the same thing. So her plan was to distract the monster with the mirror. Then Ben and Cobblestone could make their escape.

Pearl hurried to the dock's edge, where the rusty coffee can still sat. "Hello!" she called. "Hello, lake monster! I have a present for you!" But the creature ignored her. "Hey, you!"

The lake monster's head snapped around. A ray of sunlight had bounced off the pink mirror, casting a glow on the creature's face. It darted toward Pearl, slicing through the murky water like a knife, leaving two perfect waves in its wake.

Wow, it can sure move fast.

In a split second, the creature loomed overhead, its great round eyes peering down with interest.

"Hello," Pearl said with a nervous smile. The creature lowered its long neck until its face was level with the mirror. Then it blinked and stared at its reflection. A soft purring sound vibrated in its throat. *Great!* The plan was working.

"That's right," Pearl told it. "It's another lake monster, just like you. It's a friend." The monster's purring grew louder.

"Pearl!" Ben yelled. "What are you doing?"

"I'm saving you—that's what I'm doing! Start swimming!"

And that was when Pearl came to realize that sometimes plans don't always go as...planned.

The lake monster snorted, then opened its mouth, revealing a row of sharp teeth and a glistening green tongue. And before Pearl could say "Hey, have you ever thought about chewing on some breath mints?" she was lifted into the air.

"Whoa!" she cried, her stomach clenching. Then she realized that she was riding in the mouth of a lake monster, which was a pretty cool thing indeed. At least the monster didn't spin like the Whirl-a-Tron at the Milkydale County Fair. She stared worriedly at the hospital. Fortunately, no faces appeared in any of the windows. She held tight to the mirror in one hand, the golden pot in the other. As the creature picked up speed, its little teeth prickled through the waistband of her basketball shorts. Just as she thought she might forget how to breathe, Pearl landed on the beach with a plop.

Ben rushed to her side. His short hair was drenched in monster slobber. "Where's Mr. Tabby?"

"We don't need Mr. Tabby, because I have a plan," she said, scrambling to her feet.

"A plan?" Ben's voice got kinda screechy. "A plan? Your plans are terrible. You took a leprechaun out of the hospital. A *sick* leprechaun." Right on cue, gold dust sprayed out of Cobblestone's nose. "What if he gets sicker?"

"I know, I know," Pearl interrupted. "You don't have to yell at me."

Ben snapped his mouth closed. "I'm not yelling," he said between clenched teeth. "I'm pointing out the fact that this is a big mess. I should have listened to my grandfather. He told me you were a trouble-maker."

Tears stung the corners of Pearl's eyes, but she held them back. "That's a really mean thing to say."

"You're the one who talked me into leaving the hospital. And you're the one who brought Cobble-stone outside. And now we're all stuck on this stupid island." The leprechaun grunted in agreement.

Pearl stepped aside as the lake monster lunged for the mirror. "Well, maybe that's all true, but I'm going to fix things," she announced. She walked over to the leprechaun and set the golden pot at his feet. "I brought this present for you," she told him. "I'm sorry I took your gold."

He dabbed his nose with his handkerchief. "This be a present for Cobblestone?"

"Yes. For Cobblestone's gold."

"But Cobblestone's gold be across the lake," he said with a scowl.

Pearl sidestepped again as the monster tried to grab the mirror. "We're going to get back across the lake because I brought something special." She held up the mirror. The monster immediately calmed down and stared, entranced by its green reflection.

Ben folded his arms and looked from the mirror to the monster and back to the mirror. "I don't get it."

"It's lonely," Pearl explained. "That's why it brought you here. But now it thinks there's another lake monster on the island, and so it might let us go."

"Might?" Ben asked. "*Might* let us go?"

"I can't be sure, but I think it will work." Pearl started walking down the beach, holding the mirror aloft. The creature paddled alongside, its graceful neck keeping pace with Pearl. Pearl stopped at the trunk of a huge pine tree. "We'll put it here," she said.

Ben and the leprechaun wandered over. "Can we use your hammer?" Pearl asked, pointing to the leprechaun's apron.

The leprechaun shook his head. "Human hands never touch Cobblestone's hammer."

"Then will you hang the mirror?" Pearl asked. "It might be our only chance at getting off this island and back to your gold."

With a grumble, the leprechaun pulled his hammer from his apron, along with a little nail. "Very

well. Cobblestone will oblige." Ben knelt, and the leprechaun climbed up onto his shoulders. The monster watched as the little guy hammered three times, driving the nail through the pine tree's bark. Pearl handed up the mirror. As soon as it was in place, the leprechaun scrambled down.

Green scales undulated as a shudder ran up the monster's neck. It smiled into the mirror and chirped. The sound was just like the one Lemon Face made when he talked to his reflection.

"It's working," Ben said with surprise.

"Let's go," Pearl whispered.

Ben was the first to hit the water, Pearl close behind. By the time she'd waded up to her knees, Ben was already halfway across. "Come on, Cobblestone," she called.

The leprechaun held tight to the plastic pot. He pushed through a small patch of lily pads, then stopped to sneeze. Pearl cringed. Could swimming make his head cold even worse? She hadn't considered that. And all his tools looked really heavy. Maybe her plan wasn't so great after all.

"Uh, Cobblestone," she said. "Don't you think you should take off your apron?"

He stepped deeper. The water reached to his chest and then...

...he disappeared.

Leaving only the plastic pot at the surface.

17

SINK OR SWIM

Pearl inhaled deeply, then dove into the murky water. Her flip-flops floated away, but she didn't care. Where was he? Kicking, she pushed forward. *Please, please, please*, she thought as she reached in front, then to both sides, grasping lily-pad stems between her fingers. A fish bumped into her hand, then swam away. Just as she was about to run out of air, she found something solid.

She pulled with all her might. He was so heavy. Up, up, up she pulled until they burst to the surface. Gasping, Pearl and the leprechaun lay in the shallows next to the island. "Your apron," she said

between deep breaths. "You can't swim in it. It's too heavy. You'll have to leave it here."

"Cobblestone will never leave his tools," he declared. His big, round ears poked out from his drenched hair.

"But we're so close to escaping," she said, wiping a piece of lily pad from her face. "Can't you buy new tools?"

"These tools be ancient." He sneezed and water shot out of his ears. "These tools are the reason why Cobblestone be the best cobbler in all the Imaginary World."

Having reached the other side, Ben climbed onto the dock and stood at the edge, his lab coat clinging to his shivering body. "What's going on? Hurry up!" he called. The lake monster didn't seem to care one bit that Ben had escaped. It continued to chirp at its reflection.

Pearl's mind raced. There had to be some way to get across the lake with the heavy apron. That's when she noticed the plastic pot, floating past. She reached out and grabbed it. "Put your apron in here," she said. "We can push it across."

The apron fit inside, along with the leprechaun's boots. As they swam, he and Pearl took turns pushing the pot. The lake monster paid no mind, smiling, toothy green, at its reflection.

Once they'd reached the opposite shore, Ben helped them out of the water. The leprechaun put on his boots and apron, and poured his gold coins into the plastic golden pot. "Cobblestone likes his new pot," he said. Then he started coughing.

"We need to get back," Ben urged.

Pearl couldn't agree more. Barefoot, she led the way. The leprechaun carried his gold as if it weighed nothing more than a handful of feathers. It seemed silly to Pearl that the leprechaun rated a level three on the danger scale. He hadn't been one bit dangerous. But maybe that was only because his magic had been clogged by sniffles and snot.

They slipped into the hospital and rode the conveyor belt back to the Steam Room, where the air was warm and mentholated. The leprechaun sneezed three times in a row. Water dripped from the apron's soaked leather, and he began to shiver all over. Pearl found a blanket in the closet, but it didn't warm him up. "He's really sick," she said.

"Yeah," Ben agreed. "I don't feel so well, either." He sneezed, and Pearl couldn't believe her eyes. Gold dust shot out of Ben's nose!

"Wow," she said. "How'd you do that?"

"I don't know." His nostrils sparkled as if he'd

stuck his face into a bowl of glitter. "But that was pretty awesome."

"There is nothing *awesome* about catching a leprechaun cold," a voice said.

Pearl turned around and found herself staring at a plaid vest.

18

DR. WOO'S SPECIAL SOUP

Mr. Tabby looked down at Pearl, his eyes narrowed in a look of pure suspicion. He held tight to a tray. "Why are you soaking wet?"

Pearl stepped back. "Uh..." She almost slipped on the water that had leaked from her lab coat onto the floor. "Uh..."

"We fell in the lake," Ben said, clearing his throat to begin one of his elaborate stories. "We were clipping the sasquatch's toenails, just as you asked, when I went to look out the window. I opened it to get a better view, and that's when I dropped the toenail clippers and they landed in the lake. So we went to the lake to get them, and we fell in."

Mr. Tabby's red eyebrows pressed together. "You *both* fell in?"

"I started to fall in, and I reached out to grab Pearl's hand to stop my fall, but I accidentally pulled her in. That's why we're both wet."

"I see." Mr. Tabby curled his upper lip. "And why are you in the Steam Room, pray tell?"

Ben hesitated. He tapped his fingers against the legs of his damp jeans. "Why are we in the Steam Room? Is that what you asked?"

"Yes, that is precisely what I asked."

Pearl's mind raced. How could they possibly explain why, after falling into the lake, they'd jumped on the conveyor belt and had come to this room? "Well…" Ben shuffled. Then he smiled. "We got lost. Yes, that's it. We got lost."

It was a very good explanation. The hospital was huge, after all. But even though the last thing Pearl wanted was to get into trouble, she knew Cobblestone needed help. "Mr. Tabby," she said as she stepped aside, revealing the little shivering leprechaun who stood behind her. "I took him outside. He fell in the lake, too."

A soft growl sounded in Mr. Tabby's throat. "Why would you take the leprechaun outside?"

Pearl swallowed hard. "The truth is—"

"The truth be that Cobblestone asked the girl to take him outside," the leprechaun interrupted, and then he sneezed so hard, the blanket fell off his shoulders.

"Why would you go outside with a human?"

"Cobblestone likes this human," the leprechaun replied. "She be the only human to take Cobblestone's gold and then give it back again, with a nice new pot."

Pearl couldn't believe it. Not only had Ben tried to cover for her mistakes, but so had the leprechaun. She might have given each a hug if she hadn't been so worried. "Mr. Tabby, I think Cobblestone might have a fever. Is he going to be okay?"

Mr. Tabby set the tray on the counter. It held a steaming saucepan, a ladle, and three bowls. "Lake swimming should be avoided when one has a head cold," he said. Then he stuck a thermometer into the leprechaun's round ear. The thermometer beeped. "One hundred and fifty degrees."

"One hundred and *fifty* degrees?" Ben asked. "How's that possible?"

"Leprechaun blood is very hot. This is only a slight fever. Quite curable with Dr. Woo's special soup." As he removed the lid from the saucepan, a salty scent drifted out, making Pearl's stomach growl. After ladling the soup, Mr. Tabby handed a bowl to the leprechaun. "But without the soup, the fever might rise to a deadly level."

"Deadly?" Pearl gulped. Then she sneezed. Gold dust filled the air around her.

"It appears you have both caught the leprechaun's cold. I anticipated as much when I saw the three sets of wet footprints in the lobby. Leprechaun colds are highly contagious." He ladled soup into two more bowls and handed them to Pearl and Ben.

"It smells like my mom's matzo ball soup," Ben said. "Is it matzo ball soup?"

"It is Dr. Woo's special soup. A secret recipe. Drink."

Steam coated Pearl's face as she sipped. The taste was salty and sweet at the same time. She hadn't realized how hungry she was. Sneaking out of the hospital, running to the Dollar Store, and rescuing

Ben and the leprechaun from the lake monster must have burned a lot of energy. She drank three whole bowls. The broth instantly warmed her insides and somehow dried all her clothes, too. "Hey," she said, "my nose is clear."

"Mine, too," said Ben as he finished his second bowl.

"The sniffles and snot be gone," the leprechaun said with a smile.

"Wow, that's amazing. It usually takes a few days for my colds to go away," Pearl said. Another brilliant idea popped into her head. "If we sold this soup at the Dollar Store, we'd be rich."

"Impossible," Mr. Tabby said. "Dr. Woo's soup is not for sale." He pulled out his pocket watch. "Now that everyone is cured, it is time for you two to get back to work. Did you finish with the sasquatch?"

"No," Pearl and Ben replied.

"Then you had best complete your task before Dr. Woo returns."

"You're not going to fire us?" Pearl asked.

"Dr. Woo is in charge of this hospital. Whether

you stay or whether you go is her decision alone."
Mr. Tabby picked up the tray. "Come along."

"Good-bye," Ben said as he reached out to shake
the leprechaun's hand. "It was nice meeting you.
I'm sorry we caused you some trouble." Cobblestone
frowned, looking none too pleased about shaking
with a *human*.

When it was Pearl's turn to say good-bye, she
also frowned, but only because she didn't want the
visit to end. "Can I have your address?" she asked.
"That way we can be pen pals."

The leprechaun reached into an apron pocket
and took out a pair of shoes. "These be for you, Pearl,
the regular girl, who pulled Cobblestone and his
cobbling tools from the bottom of the lake."

"For me?" Pearl took the shoes. They were pink and soft, almost like ballet slippers. She slid them onto her bare feet. "They fit perfectly." Then she leaned close and whispered, "Are they princess shoes?"

"No," he said. "They be better. They be made by Cobblestone's own hand. You will discover what they do when the time be right."

19

SASQUATCH TOES

Pearl and Ben followed Mr. Tabby down the hall. "Can we talk to Cobblestone again later?" Pearl asked. "I have so many questions. Like, why do leprechauns make shoes? Do they make anything else, like hats or raincoats? And how come they're so small? And is there a king of the leprechauns? Are they related to gnomes? 'Cause he looks just like the garden gnomes in Mrs. Froot's garden. And do they really hide their gold at the end of a rainbow?"

"I'd like to know how to find the end of a rainbow," Ben said.

Mr. Tabby growled. "If you do not wish to test my patience, then I advise you to stop asking bothersome questions."

"But—"

Mr. Tabby spun around. "Consider yourself lucky, Pearl Petal, for today you stole a leprechaun's gold and lived to tell the tale. If the leprechaun's magic had not been clogged with sniffles and snot, then you would surely not be standing before me at this moment."

"Level three on the danger scale," Ben whispered to Pearl.

"I'm sorry," Pearl said. And she was. The last thing she'd wanted was to make a mess of things. "I won't go near a level-three creature again until you tell me I'm ready."

"Very wise, indeed."

They all climbed onto the conveyor belt, and Mr. Tabby pushed the button. He looked a bit silly sitting cross-legged in his crisply pleated pants. As they entered the tunnel, Pearl couldn't hold back her next question. "Wouldn't it be easier to just walk between rooms instead of riding on this thing?"

"We are taking this mode of transport because there are parts of the hospital that you are not allowed to see," Mr. Tabby explained. "The conveyor belt is a leftover from the factory days when it was part of the button factory's assembly line. Dr. Woo finds it most efficient for transporting sick creatures, especially if the creature is rather large and heavy."

He led them back to the lobby, then made a *tsk, tsk* sound as he looked at the front door. "Ben Silverstein," he said.

"Yes?"

"Do you remember what happened when you did not bolt the front door during your last visit?"

"Yeah, I remember," Ben said. "The sasquatch got loose." Ben's cheeks turned bright red. "Oh no, did it get loose again?"

"Fortunately, it did not," Mr. Tabby said as he slid the bolt into place. "But you must never leave the door unlocked again. There is someone who wants in—a very dangerous someone who would stop at nothing to get inside this hospital."

"Do you mean Mrs. Mulberry?" Pearl asked. "She's the snoopiest person in Buttonville."

"I am not referring to Mrs. Mulberry," Mr. Tabby said. "However, we will be installing a new front door security system. It is being shipped from Iceland." He strode over to the elevator and pushed the button. The doors swished open. "You will cease asking questions and resume your duties on the third floor."

Pearl and Ben stepped into the elevator.

"Who do you think he's talking about?" Pearl asked as the elevator rose.

"I don't know," Ben said. "And I don't want to find out."

Perhaps now was not the time, but at some point, Pearl definitely wanted to learn all about the mysterious, dangerous person who'd stop at nothing to get inside the hospital.

Up in the Forest Suite, the sasquatch lay on its back, snoring. "He sounds like my grandfather," Ben said. It took a while to find the clippers amid the thick undergrowth. Pearl carefully picked the chewed gum from the sasquatch's fur while Ben clipped. The sharp yellow shards flew through the air, embedding themselves in trees. Soon, all ten toes had tidy, short nails. The sasquatch twitched a few times but stayed asleep.

"What do you think it's dreaming about?" Pearl asked.

"Maybe its home or its family."

"I was just thinking we should stop calling the sasquatch an 'it.' Shouldn't we call it a *he* or a *she*?"

"I guess so. But which is it?"

They both shrugged and decided to ask Mr. Tabby some other time.

"What do we do now?" Pearl whispered, not wanting to wake the sleeping giant.

"We can go downstairs and get our next assignment," Ben replied. "But we'd better do it without breaking any rules. I don't want to get fired."

They stepped back into the elevator. Ben reached out to push the first-floor button when a nasal voice sounded from a speaker in the elevator's control panel. "Apprentices to Dr. Woo's office, immediately."

"Uh-oh," Pearl and Ben said at the same time.

Only one person could fire them. And that person had returned.

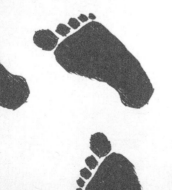

20

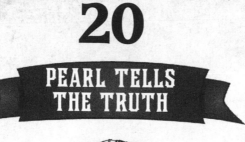

PEARL TELLS THE TRUTH

This was Pearl's and Ben's second visit to Dr. Woo's office. The room was as cluttered and messy as before, but some new items had been unpacked and now sat on the shelves, including a jar of dried beetles, a box labeled TROLL TEETH, and a glass orb that occasionally glowed. The afternoon sun streamed through the office windows, illuminating a bleached bird skeleton that hung in the corner.

"Come in." Dr. Woo was seated at her desk. Her black medical bag sat on the floor, a sprinkling of

yellow glitter around its base. She was screwing the top onto a jar that appeared to be filled with fog. "Have a seat," she said.

Once again, Ben and Pearl settled on boxes. They shared a nervous look as Dr. Woo set the jar aside. She ran her four-fingered hand over her hair, pushing stray locks from her face. Then she folded her hands on the desk and looked at Ben and Pearl, her lips pursed. Silence filled the room. Pearl fidgeted. Was Dr. Woo waiting for her to confess her crimes?

"Are we in trouble?" Pearl asked as innocently as she could.

"Who is responsible for hanging the mirror on Button Island?"

Pearl took a long breath, then squared her shoulders. "I am," she said bravely. "Ben didn't do it, so please don't get mad at him. I ran into town and got the mirror from the Dollar Store."

"You left the premises?"

"Yes." *Oh no, was that the wrong thing to say?* They weren't supposed to leave the hospital, and

Pearl had gone all the way into town. She clutched the edge of the box, waiting to hear those dreaded words: *You are fired.* But Dr. Woo just sat there, staring at her. "I thought it would help the lake monster," Pearl explained. "My parakeet, Lemon Face, loves his mirror. He thinks the reflection's another bird. And I thought that if the monster had a friend, it wouldn't feel lonely and it would let Ben go. Ben was stuck on the island. I forgot to tell you that. And the leprechaun, too. I took the leprechaun outside. I'm sorry." Pearl cringed. "I won't do it again."

Dr. Woo sat back in her chair. "A mirror," she said quietly. "A mirror to combat loneliness." Then she smiled. "That's ingenious."

Pearl couldn't believe it. She nearly fell off the box with surprise. "What?"

Ben, who'd been sitting as still as a statue, let out a sigh of relief.

Dr. Woo explained. "The lake monster has amnesia. She bonked her head on a troll's ship, and

afterward she couldn't remember who or what she was. Amnesia is terribly confusing. She started scooting around on her belly on land, making a dreadful nuisance of herself. So we brought her to the hospital for treatment. Her memories are slowly returning, but she's been very sad and very lonely. The mirror appears to have made her happy. And I think it will help her remember who she is." Dr. Woo's smile widened. "Well done, Pearl."

Pearl was used to hearing *What have you done?* But rarely had she heard *Well done.* "Thanks," she said.

Dr. Woo leaned her elbows on the desk. "And, Ben, you must have played a part as well."

"Yes, he helped hang the mirror," Pearl said. Ben nodded.

"Very good." Dr. Woo opened her desk drawer and pulled out two pieces of paper and wrote on each one. "These are certificates of merit for Curing Lake Monster Loneliness. Congratulations."

Pearl took her certificate. Ben did likewise.

"Thanks," they both said. Pearl tingled with pride. Even though she'd broken a million rules, everything was going to be okay.

Dr. Woo cleared her throat. "There is, however, another matter we must deal with." Her voice had turned serious.

It was as if all the sunshine had been sucked from the room. Pearl's shoulders slumped. "Uh-oh," said Ben. He sank back onto the box.

Trouble time.

"Do you remember signing the contract of secrecy?" Dr. Woo asked. Pearl and Ben nodded. "The contract states that you will not remove an Imaginary creature from the hospital without permission. You broke this rule."

"Ben didn't break it," Pearl said. "Ben didn't have anything to do with the leprechaun. It was all my fault."

"It wasn't *all* your fault," Ben said. "I'm the one who got grabbed by the lake monster. I'm the reason you went and asked the leprechaun for help."

"Yeah, but you didn't even want to go outside. I'm the one who talked you into it."

"Yeah, but I didn't have to go out there. It was my choice. You didn't force me."

Dr. Woo cleared her throat. "It would appear that the two of you have established a strong friendship. That will be helpful as you continue your studies."

"Continue?" Pearl said. "You're not going to fire us?"

Dr. Woo sighed. "No, I'm not going to fire you. But you will be punished for breaking the rules. Now, what sort of punishment should I assign?" She reached over and pressed a button on her office intercom. "Mr. Tabby?"

"Yes?" his voice replied.

"Do you have something particularly nasty that needs doing?"

Pearl and Ben exchanged a worried look as a long pause hissed through the speaker. What would Mr. Tabby come up with?

"Yes, I do indeed have something particularly nasty. When they come to work next, I shall assign them the task of..."

Oh please, oh please, oh please, don't make us take care of the sasquatch again, Pearl thought.

"...giving the sasquatch a flea bath."

Drat!

21

SWIMMING WITH WORMS

It was three o'clock on the dot when Pearl and Ben stepped through the wrought-iron gate, certificates of merit in hand. They'd hung their lab coats in the closet, and they'd punched out at the time clock as instructed. Mr. Tabby locked the gate behind them, then said through the bars, "Dr. Woo expects you on Wednesday at precisely eight AM."

"I'll be here," Pearl told him.

"Me, too," Ben said.

"I can't say I'm pleased with your decision to return." Mr. Tabby's lip curled in a slight sneer.

"You have proven yourselves to be overly curious and rather bothersome. But perhaps, next time, you will try to be obedient human children."

"We won't break any rules," Ben said. "You can count on us."

Pearl smiled. "Yeah, you can count on us."

"I certainly hope so." With a twitch of his mustache, he turned and hurried back to the hospital, just as Ben's grandfather pulled up in his car.

"Would you like a ride to the Dollar Store?" Grandpa Abe asked Pearl.

"No, thanks," she said. She didn't want to be stuck in the backseat of Ben's grandfather's car, not with so much excited energy flowing through her. What an adventure she'd had. She wanted to run!

"Be sure to call me and tell me if those leprechaun shoes do something special," Ben whispered to her.

"Okay," she whispered back. "You'll be the first to know."

"See you later," he called as he slipped into the

car. Then he waved as his grandfather drove off.

Pearl ran across the road, careful not to step in anything yucky. She didn't want to stain the beautiful pink leather of her new shoes. They made her feet feel light. In fact, they made her whole body feel light.

Right then and there, it didn't matter to Pearl whether the shoes were magical, because the day had been more exciting than she could have ever dreamed. She picked up the pace, then broke into a run. A lake monster and a leprechaun were now added to the list of Imaginary creatures she'd met. Who would ever believe such a thing?

But many questions remained. Why was Dr. Woo always covered in fairy dust? What had happened to the last apprentice? Who was the dangerous someone who wanted to get inside the hospital?

And the biggest question still to be answered: Where was the Imaginary World?

"Yoo-hoo!"

Pearl had just reached the edge of the Town Park

when Mrs. Mulberry's shrill voice filled the air. She stopped in her tracks to find the president of the Welcome Wagon and her daughter, Victoria, standing in the middle of a concrete duck pond. "What are you doing?" Pearl asked.

Victoria, now dressed in a polka-dot bathing suit, pulled a pair of swim goggles over her glasses. "We're looking for worms."

"That's right," Mrs. Mulberry said. Her bathing suit was striped and looked like long underwear. "I have it on the best authority that worms like to go swimming on summer days. As soon as we find one, we can make an appointment with Dr. Woo." She shooed away a duck. "Go ahead, Victoria, stick your head in the water and take a look."

Victoria frowned. "I don't want to stick my head in the water."

"Victoria, sweetie, do what I tell you to do."

"But there's duck poop."

Mrs. Mulberry put her hands on her hips and glared at her daughter. "I'm not going to let that Dr. Woo keep me locked out of her hospital. I must

know her secrets. So stick your head in the water and find me a worm!"

With a moan and then a deep breath, Victoria took the plunge.

Pearl giggled. Dr. Woo's secrets were safe and sound inside the old button factory. And they'd stay that way. She'd make certain of it. So off she ran, her new leprechaun shoes carrying her down the sidewalk and back to the Dollar Store.

And she didn't get into one bit of trouble along the way.

CERTIFICATE OF MERIT
BEN SILVERSTEIN
IS HEREBY SKILLED IN THE ART OF
CURING
LAKE MONSTER LONELINESS

CERTIFICATE OF MERIT
PEARL PETAL
IS HEREBY SKILLED IN THE ART OF
CURING
LAKE MONSTER LONELINESS

PUT YOUR IMAGINATION
≈ TO THE TEST ≈

The following section contains writing, art, and science activities that will help readers discover more about the mythological creatures featured in this book.

These activities are designed for the home and the classroom. Enjoy doing them on your own or with friends!

CREATURE CONNECTION
★ *Water-Dwelling Monsters* ★

It was once commonly believed that the world was flat, and if you sailed too far away from home, all the way to the end of the world, your ship would fall off the edge.

We laugh at such a silly thought, but it was not a laughing matter to the sailors, fishermen, and explorers who lived a long time ago. To set sail into unknown waters was scary indeed. Even after it was proven that the earth was round, there was still much to fear, for the oceans not only produced deadly storms but were also thought to be filled with monsters. On most ancient ocean maps, you'll find drawings of terrifying creatures, lurking and waiting to eat ships. Even Christopher Columbus believed these creatures to be real. So it took great courage to set sail.

Stories of sea monsters are found in most seafaring cultures throughout history. Sometimes they

are called sea serpents or sea dragons. Most often they are described as being immense in size, with long necks, small heads, tails, and fins for swimming. In the Hebrew Bible, there is a female sea monster called Leviathan. The ancient Greeks had a water monster named Scylla that waited to crush ships. The Vikings believed a sea serpent encircled the earth. All around the globe, from China to the Pacific Islands, you will find tales of these dangerous creatures.

But sea monsters aren't just found in stories. They also exist in ship logs, for many sailors throughout history have reported seeing them. And these eyewitness accounts aren't just limited to sailors. Some of the most famous sightings have occurred in northern Scotland, where people, even today, claim to have seen a long-necked monster living in a lake called Loch Ness. Locals call this monster Nessie.

Why do most seafaring cultures in the world have stories about sea monsters? Perhaps it is because the ocean scares us. It's dark and deep. We cannot breathe in it. We cannot control it. It is powerful. And so, storytellers have taken this fear and put it into a form—a monster.

But what about the people who say they've actually seen a sea monster? Scientists believe that these sightings weren't monsters but were instead giant squid, elephant seals, or even whales. In all this time, not a single monster has been captured or found onshore.

Even though the existence of sea monsters hasn't been scientifically proven, they still live on in our stories and in our imaginations.

STORY IDEAS
What do you think? Is the Loch Ness monster fact or fiction? Why do you believe this?

★ ★ ★ ★ ★

Imagine that you are the captain of a great sailing ship. You have been at sea for two months. You have never been in this part of the world before, and you are eager to find land because your crew needs fresh food and water. You are sleeping in the captain's quarters when a call comes from the deck. "Captain! There be monsters!" What happens next?

ART IDEA

Create an Old World map. Draw some continents and some islands. Then decorate the ocean with all sorts of hideous monsters.

CREATURE CONNECTION
⋆ *Leprechaun* ⋆

In the Atlantic Ocean, there lies a beautiful green island that is known today as Ireland. The Irish people are renowned worldwide for their love of storytelling, a passion that goes way back to their ancient ancestors, the Celts. Celtic stories are inhabited by conquering heroes, powerful gods, and magical creatures like fairies, also called "the wee folk." In Celtic stories, there are two types of fairies: the social kind, who love to be around other people, and the solitary kind, who always want to be alone. The most solitary of all is the leprechaun.

The leprechaun stands about two feet tall, always dresses sharply, and wears his apron, for he works as a cobbler (also known as a shoemaker). He gets paid for the shoes in gold, and he keeps his gold close by his side or hides it. Because he wants to be left alone and because he tries his best to avoid humans, he is a difficult fairy to find. The best way to find him is to look at the end of a rainbow or to listen for the sound of his little hammer.

According to legend, if a human takes a leprechaun's gold, he or she can demand that the leprechaun grant a wish. But leprechauns are very smart and tricksters by nature, so most of the time the human ends up without the gold and without a wish.

This tradition of granting wishes is found in Arabic folklore in the form of a genie who, if captured, will also grant wishes.

Today, many people recognize the image of the leprechaun, with his beard and large top hat. Usually dressed in green, his image is used on greeting cards and decorations to help celebrate St. Patrick's Day. And guess what? According to tradition, there are no female leprechauns.

So the next time you're walking in the woods, keep your ears tuned for the sound of a little hammer, and you might just catch a glimpse of the solitary fairy called the leprechaun.

STORY IDEAS

You are on assignment for your school newspaper. You need to interview a leprechaun. But leprechauns aren't easy to find because they are very good at hiding. What clues will you look for? You have to be trickier than he is, so how will you catch him?

★ ★ ★ ★ ★

You are a leprechaun, and you have been asked to make a pair of shoes for the fairy queen. These must be the most special shoes in the world. What kind of material will you use? What will the shoes look like? What special powers will the shoes have?

ART IDEA

Create your own Pot O'Gold board game. Make gold coins, leprechauns, and rainbows out of cardboard and color them. Get a pair of dice. Draw a path with a starting square and a finishing square. Make up rules. For example, if you land on a gold square, you get a gold coin. If you land on a black square, you have to go back to the start. The leprechaun who gets the most coins wins.

SCIENCE CONNECTION

★ *Why Do Some Things Float* ★ *and Some Things Sink?*

When Cobblestone the leprechaun tried to swim across the lake, he was pulled down by the weight of his tool-filled apron. This was no big surprise. The apron was heavy and heavy things don't float. Heavy things, like rocks, sink to the bottom.

But wait a minute—if that's true, then how does a heavy object like a wooden rowboat float? How does a huge object like a ferryboat float? And why did the tool-filled apron float when it was set inside a plastic pot?

Let's start with something we all know is good at floating: a rubber duck. If you place a rubber duck in your bath, you will notice that it doesn't sit on the water's surface—part of it is actually under the water. As the duck settles, it pushes away water until the amount of water that it has pushed weighs exactly the same as the duck itself. The scientific word in this situation is *displacement*. The duck has taken the place of the water, and thus the water has been *displaced* by the duck. Because the duck and the displaced water weigh the same, floating occurs.

Now take a marble and set it on the water's surface. The marble is heavy, and because of its small, round shape, it can't push away enough water to match its weight. Thus it sinks to the bottom.

There's a way to make the marble float, however. Go into the kitchen and get a plastic bowl. Place the bowl on the water. Now set the marble inside the floating bowl. The bowl may sink a little, because of the added weight, but it will continue floating. The shape of the bowl has allowed it to push away enough water to match the additional weight of the marble.

Shape is very important when it comes to floating. Cobblestone's apron sank to the bottom of the lake not only because it was heavy but also because it was soft and basically shapeless. But Pearl put it into a plastic pot that was wide and hollow, and had a solid shape, allowing enough water to be pushed aside to match the apron's weight.

So now when you see a boat traveling across the water, you will better understand why it is shaped the way it is—so that lots of water can get pushed aside.

EXPERIMENT IDEA
See how many marbles you can add to a plastic bowl before it sinks.

CREATIVITY CONNECTION
★ Make Your Own Mirror ★

There are two ways to make a mirror—the hard way and the easy way.

Most mirrors we use today are known as back-silvered mirrors. A sheet of aluminum is cut and polished in a factory, and then it's set behind a thin layer of glass. The glass protects the aluminum from being scratched. But for our purposes, a sheet of polished aluminum is expensive and difficult to work with.

What about aluminum foil, you ask? Even though you probably have a roll in your kitchen, it won't work well for this project, because it's not shiny enough. And it gets crinkled too easily.

So let's make a mirror the easy way.

Go to your craft store and buy the following things:
1. A small wooden picture frame. The frame should contain a piece of glass and a piece of cardboard.

2. A plastic mirror sheet. This can be found in the mirror section of the craft store. It doesn't cost very much, and it's easy to cut and work with.

3. Craft glue. (You might already have some at home. If your parents own a hot-glue gun, you can ask them to help you.)

4. A tube of acrylic paint—you choose the color. Look through your supplies at home.

5. A paintbrush. I bet you have an old paintbrush lying around. If not, get one.

★ ★ ★ ★ ★

Take the frame apart. Carefully set the glass aside. Peel the protective wrap off the mirror sheet. Careful, don't smudge the mirror with fingerprints.

Lay the piece of cardboard that came with the frame onto the back of the plastic mirror sheet.

Trace around it, and then cut the sheet to match the cardboard. Now you have a mirror sheet and a piece of cardboard that are the same size.

Paint your picture frame, and let it dry for at least an hour.

Reassemble the frame by setting the glass into place, then the mirror sheet, followed by the piece of cardboard.

Now you can decorate your frame however you'd like. Look through your junk drawers. You can glue on bottle caps, beads, or sequins. Go outside and find small rocks, seeds, maybe even snail shells. If you are using a hot-glue gun, be sure to get an adult to help you. Regular glue works great, too.

Handmade mirrors make great gifts. Have fun!

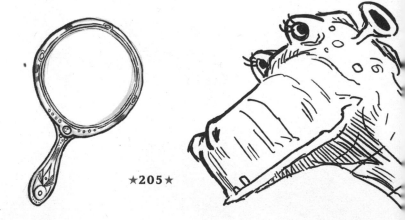

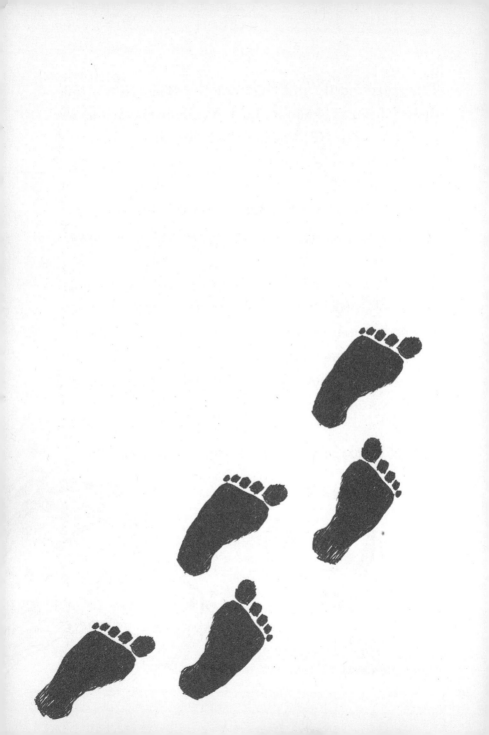

DON'T MISS THE NEXT ADVENTURE

SUZANNE SELFORS

THE RAIN DRAGON RESCUE

THE IMAGINARY VETERINARY: BOOK 3

COMING JANUARY 2014

Turn the page for a sneak peek!

1

NIGHT NOISE

It sounded like claws scratching against the side of the house.

Giant claws.

Ben's eyes flew open. *Where am I?* he wondered. The room was inky black, thanks to a pair of heavy curtains that blocked the moonlight. The mattress felt lumpy, and the quilt smelled like mothballs. Only one thing was recognizable—the soft gnawing sound of Snooze, Ben's hamster, as he chewed a toilet paper tube. It wasn't unusual for Snooze to be wide awake in the middle of the night. He was nocturnal, after all. But the other noise?

Screeeeeeech.

Had a window just opened?

Ben sat up and clutched the pillow to his chest. As his eyes adjusted, he remembered that this wasn't his regular bedroom. No glow-in-the-dark stars on the ceiling, no dinosaur-shaped nightlight in the corner, no mother or father down the hall to ask, "What's going on out there?" This was the cramped, extra bedroom right next to the kitchen at his grandfather's house.

And the noise had come from...*the kitchen.*

Back in Los Angeles, Ben's father had installed a high-tech home-security system. If anyone tried to break in, alarms would ring and guards would come running. But Grandpa Abe didn't have anything like that. The only alarm system was his black tomcat, Barnaby, who hissed when disturbed.

Hissssssssss.

Uh-oh.

Ben froze. Maybe it would be best to stay in bed.

If a burglar had decided to take something from Grandpa Abe's house, then so be it. What could Ben do? He wasn't any good at karate or judo, and he certainly didn't know how to use a lasso. The only time he'd gotten into a fight was when he wrestled Eli Finklebaum to the ground after Eli had cut in front of him, for the umpteenth time, in the snack line at school. It'd been bad enough having to wait ten minutes to get a bag of chips, but to have Eli snicker and push his way to the front every single day was totally unfair. And when he took the very last bag of Barbecue Curlies, the one Ben had been craving—well, it was an event that the students at Oakview Hebrew Academy still talked about.

Whoooosh.

A sudden burst of orange light glowed beneath the bedroom door, then disappeared. Ben sniffed. Smoke!

He scrambled out of bed. If there was a fire in the kitchen, the door would feel hot. But it was cool to his touch, so very carefully, he cracked it open.

Moonlight trickled in through the front windows.

Barnaby stood on the table, surrounded by dirty dishes, his back arched, his fur sticking up as if someone had rubbed a balloon all over it. Tendrils of smoke rose from a singed hole in the tablecloth. Barnaby stared at the counter, hissing like a snake. Ben poked his head out of his bedroom just far enough to get a better view.

At Grandpa Abe's house, the kitchen window was always left halfway open so Barnaby could come and go as he pleased. But on this night it had been opened all the way. And someone was reaching through.

Correction—not someone. Some*thing.*

The intruder's arm was covered in black scales and was long enough to stretch down the counter. Its paw, which was bigger than a Frisbee, had four fingerlike claws.

If it hadn't been for all his adventures over the last few days, Ben might have thought he was going crazy. But he knew, without a doubt, that the creature reaching into his grandfather's house in the

middle of the night was a dragon. A real, living, fire-breathing dragon. Ben had seen it before, but never up close. A brave person might have said hello. But Ben would never describe himself as brave. And talking to a dragon in the middle of the night felt risky. "You're a cautious boy," his mother always said. "There's nothing wrong with being cautious."

Ben pressed against the wall, his heart flip-flopping as the dragon's claws tapped along the counter. The dragon grabbed a bag of bagels, then tossed it to the floor. It shoved aside a roll of paper towels and a ratty old rag. It moved over plates, around coffee cups, then paused at the toaster. With a quick yank, it pulled the cord from the wall socket and whisked the toaster right out the window. Outside, a shape moved toward the front lawn.

Ben ran to the living room, climbed onto the couch, and peered out the front window. Barnaby stopped hissing and scampered up next to Ben. They both watched as the massive dragon galloped across the grass and took to the sky. Moonlight glinted off the toaster as the creature rose above the rooftops and disappeared from view.

Ben turned and glared at Barnaby. "You saw nothing," he told the cat. "That dragon is our secret."